SNARED BY THE SNAKE

BOOK 6

BARBARA BARRETT

ISBN: 978-1-948532-62-4

This book is dedicated to the plumbers of the world, who provide a service the rest us can't do without. In particular, this book is dedicated to the women who have taken on this profession, like one of the main characters in this story, Harper Wickersham.

Only after I finished this story did I learn that the busiest day of the year for plumbers in the U.S. is the day after Thanksgiving. Without giving away the plot, I'll just say how pleased I was to learn this, as it does relate to part of the story.

CHAPTER 1

"Do we really have to go to this dinner?" I asked my recently moved-in boyfriend, Chuck Dawson. The "dinner" in question was a Thanksgiving get-together my daughter, Valerie Kowalski, and her man, Jim Watkins, were hosting next door in her half of the duplex we shared.

"I can't believe you're even asking that question, Ro," Chuck replied.

I'm Rowena Summerfield, my daughter's partner for almost four years in Nailed It Home Renos. I'm also a former homicide cop grounded by a terrible car accident and a widow now in my late fifties. On occasion, I'm still called upon to investigate homicide cases as a consultant to my old employer, the Shasta Florida Police Department, working with my former partner, Hercules "Herc" Morgan. At those times, Jim Watkins—Captain James Watkins—is our boss.

"Val may have gotten past her anger with Jim, but I need more time to forgive Herc and Jim," I said.

Not too long ago, Chuck and I agreed to help my friend and project superintendent, Ryder Tompkins, find a sister he'd only recently discovered existed. In the course of our search, we learned she was running from a crooked businessman in Atlanta who was out to kill her after she witnessed him murder her date. Eventually, he was caught and killed here in Shasta, but not until Ryder and I had been used as bait by both Jim and Herc to draw him to town. Although I realized I was never in danger—they would never let matters come to that—I resented being used.

I knew all along I'd get over my hurt feelings eventually, but thus far, even though I'd spoken to both when necessary since then, we hadn't actually reconciled.

Although Val had also been upset with Jim for his part in using me as bait, enough to kick him out of her side of the duplex temporarily, Val and Jim were pretty much back to the same relationship they'd shared before Chuck and I set out on our journey. Now she wanted the rest of us to get past our issues as well and celebrate the holiday together.

The man of my life, still a hunk in his middle years at six foot plus with his short, graying, sandy-brown hair, set aside the wine carrier he'd brought from his wine bar and studied me. "I know you, Ro. It isn't like you to continue to harbor these hard feelings. There's something else behind your not wanting to go."

Chuck had come to know me pretty well. "I'm not good at hiding my feelings, which I'd have to do. It's Thanksgiving, the day we take time to be grateful for everything in our lives. I am grateful we found Ryder's sister and that the two of them have hit it off so well. Both of us could've played along with the scheme to get the killer to reveal himself. But we weren't given that chance. I was not the least bit grateful to have been left out of that decision."

Chuck placed his hands on my shoulders, his remarkable brown eyes gazing deep into mine. "I'm angry for both of you, but since I wasn't even involved, I have more distance and perspective about how things worked out." In all truth, I'd done the same thing to him that I was so upset about Jim and Herc doing to me. I'd left him out of that final scene. The difference was that I was a trained professional despite being retired. Chuck was a civilian and very special to me. I didn't want to put him in danger. Some might describe that as a rationalization, but I didn't see it that way, and fortunately, once I explained, Chuck understood.

He checked the time. "We've got five minutes before we'll officially be late. How can I help you get past your feelings, at least for today?"

"I'm not trying to make a statement. I just don't feel I can reach that deep within myself to make nice with anybody but you today."

He grabbed two potholders, removed the pan of dressing from the oven and placed it in a carrier. He'd brought it home from his restaurant, The Sandpiper, the night before. The aroma drew our tuxedo house cat, Jason, away from his resting spot, a window seat where he takes in the morning sun.

Chuck bent to pet him. "Don't get excited, guy. This isn't for you." Then he turned back to me. "Did you listen to your last sentence? 'Make nice with' your 'two friends'? Just be yourself. Don't let Val down."

I made the decision I knew all along I'd make. "All right, I'll go. But I'll be honest about where I still stand." And since that came out more petulant than I'd intended, I attempted to soften it with an offer. "You've got your hands full with the wine. I'll take the stuffing."

He screwed up his lips, like he wanted to say more but thought better of it.

Since it was a special occasion, we went to the front door of Val's side of the duplex rather than the back door we usually used. She greeted us in a cocoa-brown midi dress and bib apron, her dark locks drawn back in her customary ponytail. "Happy Thanksgiving, folks!"

"Same to you," Chuck returned as he held the wine carrier out to her.

"Ooh! You brought the good stuff. Let's have some of that now. I'm ready to start celebrating."

"That was the idea," Chuck returned.

They went off to the kitchen to uncork the wine. That left me standing there alone holding the pan of stuffing, attempting to decide what to do next.

"Happy Thanksgiving, Ro." Jim, just as tall as Chuck, entered the room. With flecks of gray competing with his otherwise dark hair, no doubt earned from the pressure of being chief of police, he was every bit the welcoming host.

I forced a smile. "The same to you, Jim." I tried to keep my tone as friendly as I could muster.

"Haven't seen much of you lately. You've been missed." He knew exactly why I'd kept my distance because I told him as much right after the case had been resolved. But he was attempting to take the high road.

Moment of truth. "I've needed the space. In fact, I'm here today because it's Thanksgiving and my daughter is going out of her way to make this day pleasant for all of us. I still need time to heal, but Chuck thought coming here might help that process along." Not exactly what Chuck had said, but I was pretty sure that was what he had in mind.

Jim nodded. "We'll do what we can to make that happen. We're happy you're here." Only then did he appear to notice I was still holding the pan. "Here, let me take that from you."

As a result, I stood there empty-handed, staring at a painting on the opposite wall, a seascape. That was new. And totally so not my daughter's taste. Must be from Jim. She was more into horse pictures. Don't ask me where that came from. She'd never ridden in her life.

Val returned to the room, a glass of wine in her hand.

"Is anyone else coming?" I asked.

"Ryder and his sister are celebrating with his mother at the care facility, although she probably won't recognize him. Her Alzheimer's has progressed," Val replied.

"We knew it was inevitable but still hard to hear," I said, keeping the small talk going even though it had taken on a more serious tone.

Jim had returned to the room during that exchange with his own glass of wine. "Herc is also coming," he said hesitantly.

"By himself?" Normally, I would've known this, but I hadn't spoken with Herc either since the night the killer was caught.

"Uh, no. He's bringing a guest. I think you've met her. Luann Cory? She's the assistant fire chief."

So Herc had followed my advice and approached the woman he'd been dreaming about for weeks, although he kept denying any interest whenever I'd asked. All I'd suggested was to send her flowers thanking her for her assistance with a prior case. Somewhere along the way he'd gotten to know her enough to invite her to this dinner. Now I wished I wasn't still upset with him because this was a big deal. Though there'd never been anything romantic between the two of us, at least on my part, Herc had been jealous of my growing relationship with Chuck until just recently. He still wasn't keen on Chuck's moving in, but he seemed to be accepting it.

Maybe I could relent just enough to get all the details. The last I knew, he was building up his courage to send that thank-you note. Apparently he'd gotten well beyond that point.

"Here you go," Chuck said, returning with a glass of wine for me, doing his part to relieve me of having to talk to Jim. "Would you mind helping me a bit in the kitchen, Mom?" Val asked, sensing my unease.

Escape beckoned. I followed her into the kitchen. "Sure. How can I help?"

"How 'bout whipping the cream for the pie? I'm afraid I'll take it too far and make butter."

"No problem." I made short work of placing the beaters into her hand mixer and finding a small bowl for the whipping cream.

"I'm glad you decided to come today," she said, joining me at the counter.

"I didn't make up my mind until just before we came."

"I kinda thought that might be the case. But I couldn't let this day go by without attempting to get the most important people in my life together."

"Thanks for trying to mediate. I don't like feeling like this, but that's the way it is. For now, anyhow."

"That's what I've tried to tell Jim once we were speaking to each other again. You and I are alike that way. It takes us a while to get past our feelings if we've been hurt. Look how long it's taken me to get past being betrayed by my straying husband, Larry."

"You still haven't, Val. You've just decided not being married to him works to your advantage now that Jim is in your life. I told Chuck and then Jim that I'll be civil today. I respect the holiday. That's all I can promise."

"Got it, Mom." She leaned over and hugged me. "Drink up."

CHAPTER 2

By the time Herc and his date arrived, I'd finished my first glass of wine. It had improved my outlook considerably, especially since I could chat freely with Luann even though I was still reserved with Herc.

"How long have you and Herc been seeing each other?" I asked. Perhaps a bit forward, but I wasn't ready to ask Herc and I was curious.

"Oh, we aren't seeing each other, at least not like you mean," she replied good-naturedly. "We were having coffee one day last week and the subject of Thanksgiving came up. My family lives out of town, so I'm usually on my own for the day. Herc asked if I'd like to enjoy a full turkey dinner for a change as his guest today. How could I refuse? Especially since he assured me I didn't need to bring a thing, although I did bring flowers."

I was accustomed to seeing the woman in her firefighting gear. I hadn't realized how tall she was. About five-eight. Not overweight but of sturdy build. She'd have to be to handle all that equipment. She wore her light brown hair short, just below her ears. That probably worked best with the helmet she had to wear.

"We're glad you could join us," I said, meaning it.

Chuck and Herc made themselves comfortable in front of the TV watching some football team play another football team. Jim joined them intermittently, when he wasn't in the kitchen checking on the turkey. Luann and I helped Val finish up the rest of the meal. Inhaling the traditional scents of Thanksgiving plus working with my hands helped me relax further. By the time we settled at the dinner table—which Val and maybe even Jim had outdone themselves decorating—my mood had mellowed to the point where I could be fairly civil.

Herc and Jim talked sports at first, such as who would win the game they'd been watching and their predictions for a national football champion. Luann complimented Val and Jim on the meal and the tablescape. Then Herc asked Val how our current projects were progressing.

"We ran into a bit of a delay with the flooring for both the residential/commercial fashion boutique as well as the mini-mansion where we've been converting two rooms into studios for the in-house artists. Then the woman who is establishing the boutique decided she also wanted to design and fabricate her own line. Fortunately, Mom figured out how we could move the design part to a small area of the second floor along with the rest of the living quarters without any other major changes."

"That was actually easier than reuniting the two artist lovers whose latest tiff threatened to call off the whole project," I said, relieved Coral Neely and Nate Bligh were once again talking to each other.

Luann looked at me like she was just seeing me for the first time. "I didn't realize home renovation involved so many more skills than simply choosing paint colors."

"Even paint colors can be a pain," Val said, laughing. "I remember a time not so long ago when instead of ecru I ordered eggplant for one of our projects and the vendor refused to take the paint back. Mom really stressed over that one until she decided to make it a feature wall."

"If all now goes as planned, we'll be done with both renos in the next week. In the meantime, we're about to begin a new rehab this week. It's an older two-story out by Lake Dahlia. The former owner, a banker in New York State, wanted to fix it up as a weekend or holiday getaway with the idea of eventually moving here when he retired, but after his recent divorce, he decided to put it on the market."

"Lake Dahlia?" Luann said. "It's not one of those homes destroyed by fire in the last few years? I was there for a couple of those cases."

"There were more than two?" I asked, cringing because my due diligence efforts before accepting this project hadn't gone far enough to learn about these fires.

"Three in total. I was away at training during the third." She took a sip of wine before adding one more thing. "Actually, there was a fourth. Neighbors discovered and doused it before it got very far along."

"That's strange," Val said. "When I drove around the area a few weeks ago, I didn't notice any structures that had been damaged by fire."

"It's a prime residential area, as you're probably aware," Luann replied. "Buyers swooped in to purchase the ravaged properties at a lower price and were busy rehabbing them before we had a chance to perform more than a cursory review."

"Weren't you able to get stop work orders so you could finish your investigations?" I asked. Three and almost four fires in a relatively small section of town seemed suspicious to me.

"Tried, but the powers that be had other plans for me. When you're short-staffed, you have to be flexible."

And take orders, even though you might not agree. But Luann seemed to be dismissing these incidents, so I filed them away in my head. For now.

"Our property showed no sign of fire damage during my walk-throughs," I said.

"Just a lot of old furniture and furnishings that had to go before we could begin demo. With the owner's blessing, we donated some to local charities and destroyed the rest," Val added.

Herc had been hanging back from this discussion, probably because he resented the time I spent in my new career, but with the extent of Luann's interest, he must've felt he had to say something. "Sounds like a fun project."

Fun? He had no idea how many problems an older two-story with a full attic presented. But I'd vowed to make nice today, so I held my tongue.

Val didn't. "Fun? Not when we have to remove or work around the building materials and procedures of yesteryear and bring them up to today's standards."

"So fire officials like me can be assured they're safe," Luann said, only half joking. Clearly, she was trying to fit in with the rest of us. "What's the current status of the project?"

"Demo's done," Val replied. "More than we bargained for. Took an extra two days. I've decided we no longer take on any houses more than fifty years old. It's too much trouble removing old wiring and plumbing and aging building materials. They all have their modern-day limitations, but they're still durable and resistant to removal. Our crew had to wear special gloves, which were bulkier and thus harder to manipulate."

"The crew's off for the rest of the week, but next week we begin the modernization, starting with the plumbing. Electrical to follow," I said.

"Would it be okay if I stopped by to observe?" Luann asked. "Not inspect. I'd just like to get a better view of the innards of a rehabbed residence for future reference."

"We'd love that," I replied, surprised. "We always keep an extra hard hat on-site if you don't have your own. We're located at 1459 Sunburst Lane."

Luann placed the knife and fork with which she'd been cutting her turkey back on her plate. "Sunburst Lane? It's not the old Mehaffy place, is it?"

"Uh, yes," Val answered. "How do you know about it?"

"I, uh, forget I mentioned it."

My curiosity shot up. "Oh, no, no going back. Tell us about this place. I thought Val and I had thoroughly scoured the abstract and deed. Nothing strange appeared to stick out."

Luann studied her folded hands.

"Luann, what aren't you telling us?" Val asked, her curiosity level as high as mine.

Herc's guest took another sip of wine before replying. "Let me caution you that what I tell you is not based on fact or any specific cases I've handled. But over the years since I moved to Shasta, I've heard stories, more like snippets of rumors, that the Mehaffy house has a history. Strange occurrences have supposedly taken place there at different times over the years."

Val leaned in, her eyes growing wide. *"Strange occurrences? You mean like … ghosts?"*

Luann sat back, biting her lips. "I didn't use that word. I, uh, don't believe in ghosts. And I've never taken much stock in hearsay, but I thought you should know what you're getting into. There's probably nothing to it, but once you start mentioning the address to others around town or especially referring to your project as the old Mehaffy place, you may receive unexpected reactions."

"Ghosts, you say?" Chuck asked, his attention momentarily turning from sports talk.

"She didn't say," I replied. "She merely said our latest project appears to have a bit of a local reputation."

Now Jim got involved. "What kind of reputation, Luann?"

She raised her hands in protest. "Forget I said anything, all of you. I reacted to the address Rowena mentioned when I should've kept still."

"Ah, Luann, everyone loves a ghost story," Herc said. "Can't you tell us anything more? If only enough to give Ro and Val a start to their historical probe."

Her gaze checked out the other five diners. All of us had stopped eating and were staring at her. She sighed. "There apparently was more than one unexplained death in that house over the years. Later residents supposedly heard sounds coming from the attic and inside the walls. Now that you've disemboweled the house, so to speak, the sounds may stop. Or …"

"Or whoever or whatever produced such sounds may not appreciate losing their former hiding places," Jim said.

"Doo doo, doo doo," Chuck sang, finding humor in this discussion.

"Guys, I really didn't mean to turn our pleasant dinner conversation to the subject of the supernatural," Luann said.

Actually, I was delighted we'd veered off in this direction. I'd been hoping we could avoid the customary Thanksgiving topic of what we were grateful for. I wasn't sure how I'd handle that this year. "I'm glad you alerted us to those stories, Luann. It won't hurt for us to check into them. Not that I believe the house is haunted, but I want to be prepared should any of our crews get spooked."

"Haunted? Spooked? I just mentioned strange occurrences," Luann replied. "But like they say, forewarned is forearmed. A trip to the library or state historical society might be in order."

"Good idea," I replied, appreciative of her suggestion.

"Enough of this ghost business. I got us off the topic of the day, the reason why we're celebrating. Even though I'm not the host, why don't we talk about what we're thankful for instead?"

The other four diners all shot subtle glances my direction. Luann had no idea what dangerous territory she'd wandered into.

"I'll start," she said. "If that's okay?"

Val regained her aplomb. "Thank you. I guess we shouldn't forget why we're all sitting here sharing this meal. Thank you for going first."

Luann folded her hands and settled back in her chair. "I'm thankful that despite the fires that broke out in and around Shasta this past year, there were no fatalities, and I hope that trend continues into this next year."

"Thank you, Luann," Jim said. "I hadn't realized that was the case, but we have you and the rest of the Shasta Fire Department to thank for that."

"We have a good team, but we can't take all the credit. We just got lucky."

"Whatever the reason, thank you for sharing," Chuck said.

Now that Luann had said her piece, no one else spoke. The rest of us had suddenly become quite interested in our meal. Finally, Val took the lead. "I'm thankful Nailed It Home Renos has continued to grow. This past year, we expanded beyond renovating on spec. We rehabbed The Sandpiper for Chuck and built a new addition as his wine bar. We also accepted the clients we told you about earlier. I'm also thankful to have partnered up with one of the best interior designers in the area, my mom."

Tears came to my eyes on that one, but before I could reciprocate the compliment, Jim had his say. "I'm thankful that you're in my life, Valerie. You brighten every day and make me excited about coming home each night."

Val sighed. "Oh, Jim. That's so sweet."

"Yeah, Jim. Sweet," Chuck said. "Thanks for setting the bar way high for the rest of us." He must've realized what he'd said, because he quickly attempted to correct himself. "That is, thanks, Jim, for reminding me how much better my life has been since meeting Rowena. Never a dull moment with you, my dear. Our recent trip around the country searching for Ryder's sister was the most fun I've had in ages."

Those tears just wouldn't go away. I knew this sharing what we were thankful for stuff was a bad idea. Everyone was taking it seriously, laying bare some of their deepest feelings. I wasn't ready to do that.

I should've jumped in and said my part immediately so I could've kept things light and humorous. Now? Now I couldn't get by with that approach.

Herc still had to take his turn. No way would he go deep. That wasn't him. *C'mon, Herc. Make a joke of all this.*

"Guess I'm up," he said. "I don't usually do well sharing my feelings, but you've all made it difficult for me not to. So, here goes. I'm thankful the gods were on my side this past year, because a couple of times I came up against a killer who didn't want to get caught and, with Ro's help, I managed to survive as well as collar them. So, thank you, Ro, for being there for me and keeping me alive."

The tears rolled down my cheeks. Couldn't stop them. How could he do that to me, be so sincere?

Val shoved a paper napkin in my hand, and I dabbed away.

I continued to wipe my face even after I'd staved off the tears. I was stalling, trying to think what I'd say. I had to be sincere without being sincere. Val. And Chuck. I could respond to their comments honestly. Right. That's what I'd do.

"Sorry about the waterworks. I wasn't expecting such, uh, heartfelt declarations today. But since that's the pattern you've set, I'll respond in kind. I had a great partner in my former life as homicide investigator, so I was both surprised and thrilled that my own daughter and I could partner up and actually enjoy our time together. Plus do a bang-up job at it."

"Thanks, Mom," she replied.

"And Chuck, thank you for not letting me continue to put you off these last months. I've come to rely on you more than I ever thought I needed. I'm grateful for your presence in my life."

There, I followed the leader. That should do it.

But they continued to sit there expectantly, like I hadn't finished. I could deal with that. I just had to stare back at them, smile and act like I was done. Because I was, wasn't I?

"And recently, after Chuck and I had found Ryder's sister and brought her to Shasta, you, Jim and Herc, knew the danger wasn't yet over and drew the killer out. Your actions secured her freedom from fear and saw justice served at the same time. I'm, uh, grateful for your bravery and cool law enforcement minds for saving her life, Ryder's and mine."

I finished. Had I said all that? I certainly hadn't planned to.

I focused on my sweet potatoes, although there was no way I

could eat right now. I wasn't ready to glance at my fellow diners yet.

Though the clock only ticked a few times, it seemed like hours before anyone responded. Val came to my rescue first. "Thanks, Mom. Perfect way to close out our statements of thankfulness."

"I'm honored by your words, Rowena," Chuck said, his tone reverent. "You know I feel the same way about you. And more so."

Everyone else at the table had dimmed in the glow of our growing mutual feelings as we smiled at each other.

But Herc and Jim didn't remain quiet. "You don't know how much your words mean to me, Rowena," Jim said. "I'm glad we can move on from that difficult time."

"I'll add my two cents," Herc said. "As much as I valued you as a partner, Ro, I value our friendship more. Like the captain said, I'm glad we can move on."

Val must have sensed my inability to reply in this intense moment of reconciliation, because she put a bow on it. "Thank you all for sharing a little of yourselves as part of your giving thanks." She paused for effect. "Now, time for the real purpose of this get-together. Who wants pumpkin pie?"

CHAPTER 3

The following day, Val and I showed up at the Mehaffy house ready to proceed with the renovation now that the place had been cleared of its belongings and demolition of the interior walls completed. It had been months since we'd tackled a residential structure this large, although Chuck's restaurant reno and new build of his wine bar had been equally if not more challenging.

The plumber wouldn't arrive to start the rough-in until Monday. Generally, he'd do his thing before the HVAC and electrical crews appeared, so they wouldn't get in each other's way, but since these subs were used to working with each other, he'd only be on his own for a day or two before the others joined him.

Val and I inspected the pipes now that they were no longer hidden behind the walls. Val ran a gloved hand over one line. Bits of rust fell off as she did. "They'll probably all have to be replaced due to their age. I just hope we'll be able to use the existing track throughout the house for the new pipes. At least some of it. Problem is, they did things differently back then. Took shortcuts. Shortcuts we can't afford to take with our modern-day standards."

"Using the old track would certainly reduce the cost," I said, ever mindful of the bottom line, although Val was the expert in home construction.

She sighed. "The more I know about this setup, the more challenges I can see. Problems that weren't evident when we were debating whether to take on this project."

"Perhaps we were too enchanted by the idea of bringing this old treasure back to life. Now that the walls are bare, reality hits."

She pivoted away from the wall and snorted. "Drop the pretense, Mom. We both know you're as excited as I am at the prospect of bringing this old girl back to life."

"More like giving her a new life," I said, noticing the finial on the newel post cap hanging at an angle, not straight up. A chill ran through me as it came off in my hand when I touched it. "Like this." I showed it to her. "Isn't it beautiful?"

She bent to examine it. "It is, but it will be even more beautiful once it's anchored on top of that newel post again."

"One more item we need to fix." I popped it in my canvas bag, not daring to leave it around until it was time to work on the staircase.

"Speaking of which, you didn't give much credence to what Luann Cory said about the house being haunted, did you?"

Although she attempted to keep her question low-key, I could tell by the way she studied me for my response that she must believe it in part.

"I, uh, hadn't given that conversation much thought since yesterday. I guess I didn't dismiss the possibility of the place being haunted, but until we run smack dab into a ghost, I don't plan to handle this project differently."

She blew out a breath, squaring her shoulders as she did. "Good! I'm glad you feel that way too. We've had enough dead people to deal with lately, what with all the murders you've been solving."

I made a mental note to follow through on Luann's suggestion that we check out Mehaffy House ghost rumors at the library.

Whenever I could work it in. Life always got super crazy as we began a new project.

"You guys beat me here," a male voice said from behind us.

I didn't quite jump, but my body went on alert. However, after two seconds of readjustment, I realized it was only Ryder here to join in the inspection, although I hadn't known he was coming. "Early bird and all that," I replied.

"I would've told you Mom and I were coming over this morning, but I thought you and Melinda were still in Atlanta," Val told him.

"She didn't leave that much behind in her old apartment," he said. "But since she left town in such a hurry, she wanted to return and make things right with a few folks."

I had a pretty good idea who he was talking about, since Chuck and I had probably spoken with those folks not long ago when we'd gone to Atlanta to find Melinda and tell her she had a brother, well, half brother, she never knew existed. Her former building manager had tried to stave off two goons who had come looking for her and had been sent to the hospital as a result. After they'd forced him to let them into her apartment, he'd had her place rekeyed as one of his parting shots before he quit. Her dry cleaner had tipped us off to the fact she was in danger when he revealed she'd left a bloodstained cocktail dress with him for cleaning.

"How was she? Going back to all those memories?" I asked.

"Quiet at first. Almost shy about showing me around her old stomping grounds. But she warmed up when she introduced me, her *brother*, to those we met." I'd never seen him wear such a broad smile. "By the time we were headed home, she was in much better spirits. I think it was a good idea for her to say goodbye to her old life. Thank you for suggesting it."

"It needed to be done. Now she can move on, look ahead to her new life, whatever she wants that to be."

"Any idea what that will be?" Val asked.

"She mentioned writing," Ryder answered. "I'm encouraging

her to take some courses at the community college, but she's been dragging her feet about them."

"Scared?" I asked.

"Probably, although she's come up with every excuse she could think of."

"Give her time. What's she doing in the meantime?" I asked.

"Trying to take care of me to 'earn her keep,' as she puts it. Her cooking skills extend to scrambled eggs and oatmeal. She's a little better at housekeeping. At least she's pretty good with a broom and making beds."

"Baby steps, my friend. We all start with tactile things when we're young. The mind develops after that. Leave some reading material lying about. When she gets bored enough, she'll start leafing through them."

He wrinkled his brow. "The only *reading material* I have is specs from various projects and construction manuals."

"Start with those. See what happens."

"She's probably trying to establish her bearings in this new environment," Val said.

"*Environment?* Listen to you, my wise daughter," I said.

"That's the right term, isn't it?"

"Well, yes, it is," I had to admit. "You sound like quite the counselor."

"Believe it or not, that's a theory I picked up working at the bank with new staff."

I turned to Ryder. "Wherever she learned it, she's right. Your sister's sharp. She could never have survived on the run as long as she did without using her brain. She just needs a chance to exercise it again."

"Thanks for all the advice," he said. "But let's talk about this project."

"Now that the place has been demoed," I said, "we have a much better picture of what we're up against. Looks like we'll have to replace more than we originally estimated."

"Yeah? That may work to our benefit. If we're not spending

all our time patching but simply putting in all new in spots, we may reduce labor costs. You and I, Val, should do a walk-through with our head plumber. Until he's had a chance to review what he's got to work with, we can't say anything definite."

Ryder went off on his own while Val and I continued to explore the house. The second-floor walls were essentially in the same condition as the first floor, although the layout was simpler, mainly rectangles, unlike the curves found in the living room and around the staircase on the first floor.

There'd been little drywall or plaster to remove from the third floor attic. What we did find were several open windows. Fortunately, it hadn't rained lately, but a few birds had found their way in. "What the …?" Val exclaimed. "How did this happen?"

"Someone has been up here, I guess. Maybe they opened the windows throughout the house during demo for ventilation and forgot the third floor when they locked up," I said.

"Looks like one of my first calls will be to a pest management control business so we can mercifully get them out of here."

"Find something to play loud music before anyone arrives," I said. "I read somewhere that's one of the more humane ways to rid your home of critters. The noise will scare them out."

"You know those costs we're trying to keep down?" Val asked Ryder when we saw him again back on the first floor. "We just added a new one thanks to one of the demo crew." She described what we'd found in the attic.

"That's funny," he replied, scratching his cheek. "I coulda sworn I went up there to check on that very thing the day they finished."

"Whatever, they're open now." She related how she was about to find a radio to blast music to encourage the exodus of the new lodgers.

Ryder shook his head skeptically. "Never heard of such a thing but might as well give it a try. Help the pest management people along."

"What aren't you saying, Ryder?" I asked as he continued to shake his head.

"I coulda sworn the place was completely closed down once demo was done. But I'll talk to the crew. Not the best way to start off a project. Good thing we're not superstitious, right, Ro?"

I chose to set aside Ryder's parting comment during the next few days, especially after the pest management people were able to clear the house of our unwanted visitors in a matter of hours. All in a very humane manner, I might add. An additional cost we hadn't budgeted for, but better than word getting out that the house had been inhabited by wildlife because our company hadn't taken the proper precautions.

Monday dawned with yet a new problem. Over the weekend, the head plumber had fallen and broken his arm and twisted his ankle, seriously limiting his mobility. Ryder found a last-minute replacement with Harper Wickersham. I hadn't run into her on a project since she'd been the one to find a dead woman on one of Ryder's home renos a few months back. I worked with Herc on that case, and she'd been one of the suspects at the top of the list. She was the one who discovered the body, at night, when the house should've been shut down for the day. As it later turned out, we learned she'd sent threatening emails to the victim when Harper's boyfriend threw her over to date the victim.

I wasn't thrilled to run into her again, but in all fairness, she had been proven innocent, at least of the murder. Like Val and me, she was a woman trying to make it in a still male-dominated business. That fact alone should be reason to try to get along with her.

"We meet again, Mrs. Summerfield," she said when I showed up that morning.

"Different circumstances, better conditions," I replied, attempting to put a positive spin on this new situation.

She didn't let it go at that. "I never got the chance to thank you for the evenhanded way you treated me when I was a suspect in the Lila Halpern murder case. Even when you accused me of lying, you were on the mark. And you gave me a chance to explain myself."

"As it turned out, you happened to be in the wrong place at the wrong time."

She grimaced. "I'll never get the vision of her broken body out of my head."

"I'm just glad we were able to find her killer," I said, attempting to put a pin in this discussion.

She apparently got the message as she returned to the wall where she'd been working when I arrived.

"How's it going?" I asked Val and Ryder, who were bent over some plans, conferring in the remains of the kitchen.

"You'd think we could go at least one day without a problem," Ryder said, huffing.

"We're fine, Mom. Just a minor glitch."

"Glitch? How minor?" I asked. How much wasn't she telling me?

"The plans have us removing that wall between the kitchen and the dining room because you want an open floor plan on the first floor. Now that the walls have been opened up, there's more going on with that one. We weren't expecting the electrical maze we found," Ryder said.

"Maze?" I understood what he'd told me, but he was deliberately generalizing his explanation. Not good.

"Apparently there were some changes made to the kitchen over the years that didn't show up in our records," he said. "Whoever made them wasn't a qualified electrician. They just stuck in the extra wiring however they could get it in."

"What does that mean for the project?" I asked. We'd run into these messed-up electrical systems in the past. Each was different. With some, it was simply a matter of rerouting the lines in a nearby wall. With others, though, it was more than rerouting due to the outdated materials used.

Val and Ryder exchanged glances. The news wasn't good if they had to signal each other before replying. "We won't know for sure until Vinny Torrance, our electrician, checks it out. He wasn't scheduled to be here today, but I prevailed upon him to stop by this afternoon."

One more sign things didn't look good. I knew better than to push for an answer at this point. Ryder didn't want to commit to any action plan until his expert inspected the situation.

"Okay, I'll wait to hear the full story until after you've consulted with Torrance. I stopped by to recheck a few dimensions for my design plan and then I'm out of here."

Val grabbed my arm as I headed off. "Mom? Don't worry about this unless it turns out you have to. This is just par for the course."

"Good luck, then." I stuck around another fifteen minutes, long enough to get my dimensions, and then returned to my office.

THE ELECTRICAL PROBLEM TURNED OUT TO BE LESS CRITICAL THAN IT could have been. More a case of first-day jitters—not unusual— which could be remedied in little time with minimal cost. Yay! I celebrated our successes as they happened, because there would undoubtedly be less successful complications ahead. Just the nature of the business.

Knowing that we'd cleared that hurdle, I arrived at the site the next day full of optimism. Time to proceed, full steam ahead. That mood lasted until I walked in the front door to be met with an apparent confrontation between our substitute plumber, Harper Wickersham, and one of her crew.

"You knew full well I'd already inspected that section of pipe." Wickersham's voice reverberated throughout the entire down-stairs. "Now you've wasted precious time duplicating my efforts."

I stopped in my tracks, listening to the little drama transpiring several feet away from me. Neither noticed my arrival.

"But Harper …"

"Boss, while you're working for me."

"But Boss, you yourself told me to go over it. First thing this morning. I was only following orders," the young plumbing apprentice replied plaintively, his hands rubbing his trouser legs.

"I did no such thing! I …" She paused mid-sentence, her mouth still open. "Now that you mention it, I guess I did say something to that effect. Sorry."

"If it helps, I found pretty much what you discovered, only more. That whole section needs to be replaced. That is, if you say so?"

"Note it on the list," she said.

The young worker shot away from her. She stood there rubbing the back of her neck. I should've moved away and let it go at that. But I didn't act fast enough. Wickersham noticed me on the sidelines.

"Sorry you had to see that. I was … out of order. Everything's fine."

"Is it?" I asked. "That run-in with your worker seemed a tad over the top."

She raised a brow. "How I treat my crew is my business."

"My comment was aimed at you, Harper. Everything okay?"

"I'm fine, I just … I shouldn't have taken my mood out on him."

"Mood?" Was the extent of this job too much for her?

"If you must know, I broke up with my boyfriend last night. Well, he broke up with me. Caught me off guard. Did it in a busy restaurant."

She shouldn't be letting her personal feelings affect her job performance, but she knew that as well as I. I'd been there myself once or twice, to my humiliation. "Maybe you should take a short break. Give yourself time to recoup your attitude?"

"Thanks, but no. I'm okay. I'll go apologize and grab some water. Don't worry about me."

She wasn't okay, but I didn't want to push it. I sensed she didn't want to be seen as a moody woman by the other men on this job. Even though there were only a few crew members on-site just yet, word had a way of getting around, especially when it concerned a woman.

I let it go. I needed to get back to my office to work on plans I was drawing up for a new proposal. I left it up to Wickersham to defuse the situation.

Wickersham failed to show up for work the next day. I got to the site just as Val was attempting to locate her.

"No word from her at all?" I asked. Had I underestimated the extent of her condition the day before?

Val shook her head. "I'm not sure we can locate another plumber at this late date."

Before I could ask if she'd let Ryder know, my phone rang. "Ro? It's Herc. I need you down here at the station as soon as you can get here."

"I'm on a job right now, Herc." This idea that he or Jim could pull me away from my renos at the blink of an eye to help them was getting old.

"This isn't about helping me on a case. The suspect has asked for you to sit in while we question her. You know her. Harper Wickersham. It would appear she offed her boyfriend after he sent her packing. She won't talk unless you come."

CHAPTER 4

"Thank you for coming, Mrs. Summerfield," Wickersham said as I was admitted to the interview room at police headquarters. Herc had met me in the lobby to escort me. His partner, Aloysius "Al" Buford, was already seated across from her.

"Mrs. Summerfield is not here in any official capacity," Herc said as soon as I'd taken a seat at the end of the table. "You said you wouldn't talk until she was here. Now she's here, so start talking about your relationship with Jed Craddock."

"Can't you tell me why I'm here first?" she asked. "Did something happen to Jed?"

Herc and Al exchanged looks. "Jed Craddock was attacked and killed sometime early last night. We understand that until recently you and he were a couple until he cut things off two nights ago. In front of several diners at The Sandpiper Restaurant."

Wickersham's complexion went even paler than usual for the blonde. "Jed killed? How?"

"We're not at liberty to say at the moment," Al replied. "We're more interested in what you know about the man."

"Wait! Before you go any further, why am I here?" I asked. I faced her directly. "I'm not on the force."

"I know," she said. "But you were so straight with me when I was involved with that other case, I wanted you here while they question me."

"I'm not an attorney, Harper. That's who you really should have here with you."

"Am I under arrest?" she asked Herc.

"Not at this point. You're here to answer some questions about the victim."

She returned her attention to me. "Thanks for the advice. I'll get an attorney if and when I am arrested. For now, I just want you here to explain things to me like you did before."

"Is that okay?" I asked Herc. He wouldn't have called me if he objected, but it seemed appropriate to ask.

"As long as you realize you're not here in a professional sense," he replied. "Now, Ms. Wickersham, let's proceed. Tell us how long you've known Jed Craddock."

"About a year or so. He worked on a few construction projects I've been on, and I'd run into him on occasion. I was seeing someone else early on in that period. Scott Sheridan. You remember him. His name came up in the Halpern case because he dropped me to date her. I started seeing Jed after that."

"Was it serious?" Al asked.

"Not really. I needed someone to stroke my ego. He was just putting in time working construction until he got on with the Sheldon Agency. Jed wanted to be a model. This local business was just the first stop on his journey to the Big Time."

"The Big Time?" Herc asked. At times, Herc could be incredibly obtuse when it came to popular culture, but I suspected in this case he knew what she meant.

"New York. He thought all the major modeling agency work was there."

"Ah. How was he doing?" Herc asked.

"I really couldn't say. The agency owner, Helena Sheldon,

apparently trains her new *finds* on-site and invited Jed to move in a few months back. He couldn't resist the offer of free room and board, plus what he thought would be constant admiration."

"How did you feel about that?" Al asked.

"I was happy for him at first. He wasn't all that great in construction. Though he had the brawn for the heavy lifting types of jobs, he really wasn't into it. He had the looks for modeling, and he was willing to spend hours at the gym getting his body in shape. But he didn't realize he'd be competing with other trainees. That discovery did not go over well with him."

Herc jotted something on his notepad. That information may or may not have had an impact on him. He sometimes did that to give himself time to consider what he'd just been told. "How do you know that was his reaction?"

"He told me, more like he complained about it often."

"Did he ever tell this Sheldon woman he was disappointed with his treatment?"

"Not that I'm aware. He didn't want to rock the boat and get himself thrown out of the program," she replied.

"Did he ever take out his frustration on you?" Al asked.

She didn't answer immediately. "He didn't hurt me physically, if that's what you're asking. Jed wasn't a woman-beater. At least not with me. But there were a few times when he'd be moody. He wouldn't talk. He just sat there playing games on his phone."

"How would you describe his general mood lately?" Herc asked.

"Cranky. Irritable. Preoccupied. I shouldn't have been surprised he called things off between us, although I thought he was sticking with me because I represented sanity on the outside. I was someone who'd listen to his problems."

"Are you saying there was no specific event or problem that ended your relationship?" Al asked.

"Not that I'm aware. We were eating dinner Monday night, and suddenly he threw his napkin on the table, stood and told me we were done. Then he left me sitting there with everyone around us staring at me or pretending not to have heard."

"And you resented him for humiliating you," Herc said, daring her to respond.

"Uh, guys," I said. "This may be where Ms. Wickersham should bring in legal help."

Herc gave me a dirty look, then his features softened. "Perhaps you're right. Want to stop long enough for you to seek legal help, Ms. Wickersham?"

"It's okay, Mrs. Summerfield. I'll answer his question. I wasn't humiliated by Jed's public rejection. I was angry. You saw me. I chewed out one of my workers for nothing. But after we talked, I went back and apologized to the crew member, which surprisingly had a soothing effect. The rest of the day went quite well. If you were insinuating I was so upset with Jed that I killed him, Lieutenant Morgan, you are following the wrong lead."

"You're a plumber, is that correct?"

"Yes," she replied. "Why?"

He nodded to Al, who reached down and pulled up a large, clear evidence bag. Inside was what appeared to be a plumber's snake. "This yours?" Al asked.

She sat back. "It could be. Is there a small black W near the bottom of the handle?"

Al viewed it through the bag, then nodded.

"So it's mine? Why do you have it?" Her voice had lost some of its intensity.

Herc addressed me. "It's time for you to leave now, Ro."

I knew what that meant. I didn't know the details surrounding Craddock's death, but the plumber's snake was somehow involved, which tied Wickersham to the crime. I could no longer be there as an observer. She now needed legal representation, whether she wanted it or not.

"You're arresting me?" Her voice ramped up again. "Just because you have my tool? I leave it in my truck. Anyone could've taken it."

"We're testing it for prints. Yours are already on file from when you were a suspect in the Halpern case. If yours are the only ones we find, we'll have a pretty tight case against you." He left it at that.

"And then what?" she asked. "If someone was smart enough to remove it from my truck to frame me, it stands to reason they'd also wear gloves so only my prints would remain."

She had a point. The fact it appeared her tool was the murder weapon was damning evidence but not conclusive. Herc knew that, but for now, it was the strongest lead he had.

He squared his shoulders, as much as that was possible for a man who was out of shape. I knew that move. He was shifting into high cop mode.

I was only there as an observer, but this was too much, too fast, as Wickersham had pointed out, based purely on the fact she owned the tool. Anyone could've taken it. He hadn't even determined if she had an alibi yet. "Wait," I said, forgetting I was there only to observe. "You haven't asked her about her whereabouts around the time the murder was committed."

Herc looked at me like he might want to commit his own murder right now. But he took a breath and then asked her for her whereabouts the night before.

"I stayed late at Mehaffy House. Till at least six thirty. Probably a little later." She turned to me. "I was sorry I'd behaved so poorly around my crew member earlier in the day. Especially since you overheard me, Mrs. Summerfield. That's not my style. I worked a longer shift to redeem myself. Check with your daughter. She was still there too."

I shifted my gaze to Herc. At this point, I had no idea when he thought the murder had occurred. "And the rest of the evening?" he asked next. "Did anyone see you then?" He wasn't ready to reveal the time of death just yet, which meant her alibi wasn't enough to clear her.

She considered. "I was still feeling sorry for myself, so I treated myself to a pizza. I ordered it before I left the project and picked it up at Arturo's on my way home. After that, I went back to my apartment and pigged out on the pizza. I watched some rom-coms on TV, trying to take my mind off the breakup." She seemed to realize how important her response could be. "When do you think he was killed?"

"We're not at liberty to say at this time," Al replied. He exchanged a look with Herc.

"Thank you for coming in, Ms. Wickersham," Herc said to her. "You're free to go, but we may have follow-up questions for you once we're further along with the investigation."

She and I left at the same time, although we turned to go different directions when we reached the outside door. "Thank you for coming in, Mrs. Summerfield," she said before I could escape. "I might've been behind bars by now if you hadn't."

"Don't thank me yet. The snake they showed you could be pretty damning evidence. You might want to find a good criminal attorney just in case."

"Do you think it could come to that?"

"I don't know any of the specifics of the case. An attorney might be able to learn some of them"

"Thank you. I've got an attorney for my business. I'll ask her for a name. I still can't believe he's dead. Despite his dumping me, he didn't deserve to be killed."

I RETURNED TO MY OFFICE AND THE PROPOSAL I'D BEEN SO EXCITED about before I received Herc's call. I stared at my computer screen for the next several minutes. My brain seemed to have frozen. I kept thinking about that plumber's snake. If Wickersham had really killed her former boyfriend, why would she use that particular tool unless she was defending herself and it was the only thing handy? Moreover, if she had done the deed that way, why leave the murder weapon so conveniently nearby?

My vibes were telling me this had been a setup. Someone was

trying to frame the woman; whether intentionally or to throw the blame away from them remained to be seen.

But this wasn't my case, which was just as well, because my initial thoughts at the moment were more against than for identifying her as the killer.

CHAPTER 5

That evening, Chuck and I were enjoying a nice quiet dinner he'd had sent over from the restaurant—our leftovers from Thanksgiving that Val had sent home with us now gone—when Herc arrived. At the front door rather than his new habit of showing up at the back door.

Something was up.

"Hope you've finished eating, Ro. There's something I'd like to discuss with you."

"Actually, we're still eating. There's plenty more, if you'd like to join us?"

He thought about my offer for a few beats, then shook his head. "Not this time. Can we talk somewhere private?"

Chuck, who'd followed me into the front room to greet our guest, twisted and turned to go back to the kitchen.

"I don't mind if you stay, Chuck," I said. Our relationship had been growing progressively closer lately, and I thought he should be involved in whatever Herc had to say.

Chuck smiled at my consideration. "That's okay. I'll keep your food warm."

I expected Herc to make some sort of snarky comment about

Chuck and me, but he didn't. Instead, he found his way to the sofa and gestured for me to have a seat in the nearby chair.

This was getting serious. He was behaving too formally.

He clasped his hands and studied them briefly. "Just after you left, Al got a call from Orlando. They've run across a complicated case of two partners' intertwined finances that need to be separated and requested that Al sit in to help. Needless to say, my partner jumped at the opportunity to work with the Big Boys. His term. And Watkins got just about as excited to have one of his people working with them."

I had this terrible feeling in the pit of my stomach, but I kept silent, hoping I was wrong.

"Jim wants you to step in for Al on this case. It shouldn't take much time, because we think we've got our murderer with Wickersham. Open-and-shut case of strangling with the plumber's snake. I just need a partner."

At times, my stomach was a pretty good indicator of trouble ahead.

I attempted to skirt my feelings about this one, if possible. "You've got two crackerjack junior officers, Greg Ennis and Isla Dexter, cutting their teeth on homicide cases. Why not bring them on board to assist you?"

He twiddled his thumbs, one of his tells when he didn't want to come clean. "Watkins suggested you. Ennis and Dexter can assist, if it comes to that."

I was running out of excuses, which left me with my real feelings. "I couldn't give this case a fair hearing because I think you rushed to judgment. Had I not suggested you ask about her whereabouts last night, you weren't even going ask for an alibi. The murder must've occurred before she left the project or you would've held her at least until the fingerprint report came back."

That stopped him. Momentarily. "What are you saying?"

"You've got a circumstantial case against her at best. You just 'happened' to find the murder weapon near the body, although I didn't hear where yet. Wickersham isn't stupid. If she killed the man, even if it was in the heat of passion and she ran away immediately, she wouldn't leave the murder weapon, snake or whatever, behind." Unless it couldn't be removed from the victim. Too grisly to consider. "My take is she is being set up to take the fall for someone else, someone who stole the snake from her truck and used gloves to do the deed. It's even possible they heard how Craddock had ended things so dramatically with her the night before and took advantage of the timing."

"You talk a good line, Ro, but the evidence doesn't lie."

"You and your reliance on 'the evidence.' Evidence can be altered to suit a killer. You know that as well as I. I've always been the one to go with my gut feelings, and this time, they're telling me you haven't got the full story."

"Since you put it that way, why don't you join up with me again and help me get the full story?"

I grimaced inwardly. I'd set myself up for that. "I just started on our new project, Mehaffy House. This isn't a good time to leave Val and Ryder to handle things on their own."

"That the house we talked about at Thanksgiving?"

"Yes."

"Maybe this case came along just in time. If it's as haunted as rumor has it, your best bet is staying away from it."

"You're grasping at straws." He'd run out of good reasons for me to join him, and now he'd turned to the emotional. Even though I'd told him at Thanksgiving that I'd gotten past my anger at him for setting up Ryder and me in his sister's case, this was enough to make me reconsider.

Herc ran his hands up and down his pants legs. "Okay, Ro, you got me. Something about this case seemed too pat to my seasoned cop's instincts, even though we brought in Wickersham on the evidence we have. But Al was convinced she did it, so I let him roll with it. But he got ahead of himself with his assumption and either forgot or chose not to ask her for an alibi. Good catch. We owe you, although it's still possible she was able to pull it off within that timeframe. Possible, but tight."

"Even if Al avoided the question, it's not like you to have overlooked it. Is your mind too much on Luann Cory these days?"

He choked. "Luann? We told you the other day we're just getting to know each other."

"Perhaps not fast enough?" I said.

He shook his head. "That's not what happened today. I screwed up, that's all. The old brain let me down. Maybe I really should start giving retirement more thought."

Was he really thinking more seriously about retirement, or was his statement one more ploy to get me to join him on this case? Still, he wasn't all that determined to put Wickersham away. But I sensed he was unsure what to do about that. "Good. I'm glad to hear you aren't convinced she's guilty."

"That may be the case, but I need your help steering me toward other possibilities."

"Don't try that line on me, Hercules Morgan. You're the one who taught me how to investigate."

"The student surpassed the teacher years ago."

"Bull! You just want me to feel sorry for you and say yes."

"Is it working?"

"What do you think?"

He considered. "That you would take pity on me and agree to help."

"Try again."

"How 'bout we make a deal? I give you something you want if you'll join me."

I was about to laugh down his suggestion when an idea occurred. Not that it was on the top of my list of things I needed, but it might prove helpful nonetheless. "I want to quash the rumor that Mehaffy House is haunted. Are you willing to spend the night there on your own?"

He stared at me for several beats before blinking. "You mean, like camp out?"

"I suppose that's one way of looking at it. Are you game?"

He screwed up his eyes. "Why? Don't tell me you believe the rumors? I thought you scoffed at the idea."

"I do. But word of the house's reputation has gotten out to some of the workers on our crews. I'm concerned they may refuse to work there. If I were to stay there to prove it's not haunted, I doubt they'd believe me. But a bona fide police officer demonstrating the house is perfectly safe will go far to relieve their worries."

"You amaze me, woman. You're hesitant to camp out yourself, so you've found a way to finesse me into doing your dirty work."

He wasn't past his prime. He picked up on my ploy right away.

"Fine," he said. "You've got yourself a deal if you help me find this killer."

"Okay." I wasn't exactly delighted to be working another homicide, but it was worth it to clear up this ghost business.

"Before we move on with this arrangement, let me make this clear. I knew you'd say yes even without my stalking your ghosts. Don't think you've gotten away with anything," he declared before he left.

"What did your pal want?" Chuck asked when I returned to the kitchen.

"Take a wild guess," I said, reluctant to tell him what I'd agreed to but figuring I might as well get it out of the way.

He sat forward in his chair and set down his fork. "No! Rowena, you keep telling me you've consulted on your last case."

"He played me, appearing to charge the wrong person, in my opinion, based upon circumstantial evidence. I couldn't let that happen."

He shook his head. "Of course not."

"But I got something out of the deal too," I was quick to add. "He's going to camp out overnight in Mehaffy House to prove to everyone, particularly our crews, that the place isn't haunted."

He narrowed his eyes. "That's your new project site, isn't it?"

I nodded, still pleased with myself.

"How do you know it's not haunted?"

"What? Of course it's not haunted. I don't believe in ghosts."

"Pretty sure of yourself."

Was he pulling my leg? His reaction to my agreeing to sign on again with Herc? "Don't tell me you believe in ghosts?" I asked.

He shrugged. "Maybe. I've never run into a situation that called upon me to decide."

"Perhaps you should join Herc," I said, knowing full well the two of them staking out my house on a ghost watch would never happen.

"Perhaps I should."

"No! The whole purpose of my bargain with him was to stick him there by himself overnight."

"Punishment?"

Punishment? Really? Would I do that to Herc? "No, more like a challenge. Nothing my old partner likes better than a challenge to prove to the world he's still on top of things."

"Whatever. I wasn't really keen on camping out in the old place anyhow." He took my hand. "Now if you were to join me for our own private party, that would be different."

"No need." I raised a brow. "But I wouldn't say no to a private campout with you somewhere else."

"Ever been in a yurt?" he asked.

"One of those fancy round tents?"

"Yeah."

"Isn't that more like glamping?"

"So?"

"So that's a far cry from ghostbusting," I replied.

He grinned. "That's my point."

"Save it for another day, lover boy. Maybe to celebrate completing Mehaffy House."

CHAPTER 6

The next morning, I joined Herc in the investigation by returning to Harper Wickersham with more questions. We found her back on the job at Mehaffy House.

"I thought I answered all your questions yesterday, Lieutenant?" she said when we showed up.

"My partner, who you met yesterday, has been called away on another assignment," Herc told her. "Mrs. Summerfield has agreed to step in and join the investigation."

She offered me a courteous smile. "Mrs. Summerfield, I'm happy to hear you signed onto this investigation. With you I know I'll get a fair hearing."

I studied her more than I had the day before. She was an impressive woman. Tall, with that full mane of blond hair now pulled into a bun in work mode, she could've worked for her late boyfriend's modeling agency. I was sure her height helped her survive in the male-dominated field of plumbing.

"If we find your plumbing tool has only your fingerprints on it, that's still the most solid evidence we have," Herc told her. "But we haven't closed the case. We're still interviewing others who knew the victim."

"And had much better reasons to kill him than I had," she replied, adamantly sticking to her plea of innocence.

Enough of the preliminaries. "We're here to get more background on the man. What can you tell us about the people he associated with recently?" I asked.

She paused, like she was debating how much to share. "He had visions of becoming a top model in the next year. Visions that were nurtured by Helena Sheldon, the woman who owns the business. Her studio complex, which was once a thriving motel."

"You said he was excited when they signed him," Herc said. "Did that excitement wear off?"

"Almost the first week after he moved in, he was complaining about the way he was being treated. Somehow, he'd gotten the impression he was the only new find Sheldon had invited to live in her complex. He soon learned there were two other guys living there competing for not only the jobs she found them but also for her attention."

"Did he mention their names?"

"Trey Compton and Joel Drysdale."

"How did they get along?" I asked.

"Though Jed was disappointed to learn he had to compete with the other guys, he thought he was up to the task. But when jobs and promotional opportunities kept going to Trey, he began to distrust him."

"Anything else?" Herc asked.

She pulled on her ear. "Something happened recently that caused him to believe he would soon be released from his contract. He didn't want to talk about it when I pushed to learn more."

"What about others in his life?" Herc asked.

"The rest of his family, his parents and two brothers, live up in Indiana. I never met them, and they didn't appear to be close. I considered calling them last night but changed my mind since I was no longer in the picture. I'm the main person he met when working construction. As for friends, I may have met a few, but I can't recall their names. Sorry I can't help you more there."

"Okay, thanks for the information," Herc told her.

"Wait! Am I still a suspect?"

"Let's call you a person of interest for now. We need to learn if there's more evidence out there."

"Evidence? Someone must've known about me and what I do because they're the ones who stole my snake and used it to kill Jed."

"Thanks for the background," I told her. "We'll likely be back after we talk to others because you appear to have known him best."

"Ready to hit up this Sheldon Studio?" Herc asked once we left Wickersham behind.

"I'd like to get some more background on it first," I replied. "I've never heard of them. That seems strange for a business trying to make a name for itself."

I searched for Sheldon Studio on my notepad computer. I couldn't find much, just an address, telephone number and a graphic having very little relevance to a modeling agency.

"Want me to ask Dexter to do some deep digging?" he asked.

"Not yet. It's legit enough to have a website. Let's go find out for ourselves what goes on there."

The only experience I had with modeling agencies was what I saw on film and television, and that tended to be rom-coms or sitcoms where the owner was a handsome bachelor surrounded by a bevy of beauties, frequently in bathing suits. That probably came from the seventies or eighties, another time, another age.

The Sheldon Studio was none of that. As Wickersham told us, it appeared to be an old, converted mom-and-pop motel on the edge of town. It was built in an *L* shape. The two-story long end was made up of individual rooms. The main part, which at one time might have served as the lobby with perhaps a restaurant and a few offices, looked like it now housed some offices and the main living quarters. There was also a fenced-in swimming pool in the area in front. Maybe bathing-suit-clad beautiful people were still a part of the image.

A young woman with straight shoulder-length hair the color of onyx and dark eyes accentuated with overdone kohl makeup was parked at the front desk reading a fashion magazine. When she continued to read, Herc cleared his throat. "We're with the police, miss. Here to interview the occupants of this building."

She finally glanced up after about thirty seconds. "Thought you folks got what you needed the other night."

"Preliminary stuff. We're back to hear the real story."

"Guess you should start with my mom then. She owns this place." She drew herself from her chair and came around the desk. "Her office is down the hall. I'll take you."

Helena Sheldon, a tall, stocky redhead, remained seated once her daughter announced us, although she did put down her pen and gazed directly at us. "I told the police everything I knew the other night." She returned to her desktop computer.

"We need a little more of your time, Mrs. Sheldon, to fill in some details that weren't covered in the statement you made to the officers on the scene."

"Is this really necessary?" she asked, like a visit from the police was on the same par as a salesperson at the door.

Herc remained in his most official law enforcement mode. "Yes, actually, it is. We're attempting to find a murderer here, and your information, since you found the victim, is key to proceeding with the case." He paused for effect. "We can do this here or at the station."

She blew out an exasperated breath, but she did move away from her computer. "All right, since you must. But my time is limited. I need to finish this report."

We each lighted in a visitor chair in front of her desk, although she hadn't invited us to sit.

"Let's start with this business," Herc said. "Tell us what you do here."

She offered a blank expression. "We're a modeling agency. We find them, train them and send them off on jobs." Her reply sounded the way an impatient parent would reply to a child who asked for the hundredth time why the sky was blue.

Now Herc became the parent. The patient parent. "Yes, I get that. But who's your audience, your client base?" The man had been listening to me over the years. His questions were becoming much more esoteric.

She rolled her eyes. "We provide talent for a variety of clients, TV commercials, magazine ads, and more recently, social media."

"How many models are we talking about?" I asked.

"Until Jed's death, we had three. All young men under the age of thirty. We are somewhat unique in that we also provide training to our models as well as residential services. That way we can ensure our models follow our standard practices and are immediately available to clients."

"You're only interested in male models?" Herc asked, sparing me having to ask the question without making it sound like she was building her own harem.

"That's how it's worked out so far. It helps focus our efforts."

"How long have you been in business?" Herc asked.

"Two years. Before that, I worked at regional TV stations for fifteen years and did some modeling myself."

"You've referred to 'we' a few times," I said. "Who would that be?"

"My husband, Bart, and I run this place together, although I'm in charge of day-to-day operations. My daughter, Lola, also works here. She's the one who showed you in."

"How would you describe your relationship with the victim?" Herc asked. "Did you get along with him?"

Her mouth curled into something reminiscent of a smile. "Yes, although I haven't seen much of him lately. I've been spending my time in business meetings, many outside the complex."

"I thought you were the main modeling instructor?" I asked.

"I was when we first got underway, but I've found my skills are better used generating goodwill for the agency."

In other words, clients weren't knocking down their doors and she had to be out there hustling. "Has someone else taken over that role?" I continued.

"Bart has handled some of the training in the past, and more recently we brought Joel Drysdale on board. He's a former model from Miami."

"Your statement says you found the victim in your fitness room around seven o'clock the night before last. Is that correct?" Herc asked, returning to strictly the facts of the case.

"Yes, that's right."

"Why did you go there?" Herc asked.

"He was late to a meeting we were holding in our conference room and not returning my calls. I sent people off to various parts of the complex to look for him. The fitness room is just down the hall from the conference room, so I said I'd check there."

"Your statement says you found him doubled over the stationary bike and when you approached him, he was unresponsive. Did you touch him?"

"I touched his neck to check for a pulse and couldn't find one."

"And when you didn't find one?" he asked.

"I called 9-1-1, of course. I was pretty sure he was dead, but someone with more training needed to make the final decision."

"That's when you noticed the plumber's snake?" I asked.

"Is that what it was? I'd never seen such a thing."

"Where was it?"

"It was lying behind the bike, coiled up on the floor. That's all in my statement," she said dismissively.

Herc took another turn. "Did you notice anything else out of the ordinary, either next to him or somewhere else in the room?"

"No."

"Does your talent typically use this room in the evening?" I asked.

"Frequently. It's the only free time they have during their days, and all of them are dedicated to staying in shape."

"So it wasn't unusual for him to be there?"

"No, other than that night. Meetings take precedence."

"What was the meeting about?" Herc asked.

"That has nothing to do with his death," she returned.

It's a red flag whenever a person of interest dismisses a question. Herc cocked his head. "Perhaps. Perhaps not. Please answer the question."

She chewed a lip. "We were announcing a new compensation plan."

The second red flag went up. It was always possible she had been about to give them good news, but I suspected the opposite. The place wasn't exactly rundown, but from the look of things—torn wallpaper in the corridor, faded hall carpet, ratty-looking furniture around the pool—a potential reduction in force could have been causing tension amongst them. The kind of tension that might have prompted someone to murder one of their peers.

"Did the meeting take place?" I asked.

"No. Bart and I have put the announcement on hold until the business with Jed's death gets solved. Which I thought had taken place. Don't you already have the killer in custody?"

"Where did you hear that?" Herc asked a little too quickly. He took great pride in the department's ability to maintain confidentiality.

"One of the staff told me. I don't remember who. Word gets around. Harper Wickersham has been on-site a few times with Jed."

And there was the connection. Someone here could have known she was a plumber and about the breakup and used it against her. *Could have.* Not necessarily *did.*

"Have you ever met her?" I asked.

"Briefly."

Apparently that was all she planned to say about our current suspect. But Herc and I weren't done. "Tell us about your relationship with the victim," Herc said.

Her eyes went wide for a beat. "How do you mean? I treated him like I did the other two men."

Why was she so reluctant to give us any information? "And how was that?" I asked.

"Friendly."

"Could you be more specific?" I continued.

"There was no bad blood between us, if that's what you mean."

"How much time did you spend with him?" Herc asked.

"I don't know. Maybe a half hour a day if you added up the times we ran into each other."

"Would you estimate you spent the same amount of time with the other two men?"

"More or less. One, Trey Compton, has needed a little more attention than Jed and Joel Drysdale."

"Why was that?" I asked, feeling like I was pulling taffy.

She waved a hand. "Trey has shown a lot more potential than the other two, even though Drysdale has previous modeling experience. I couldn't let that go unnoticed. He's required more coaching, more hands-on development."

"Hands-on?"

"Not literally. Just additional time running through techniques."

"How did Jed feel about the extra time you spent with Compton?" Herc asked.

"He never confronted me directly."

This session had become quite the tennis match, as we lobbed a question to her and she vaulted back her short replies. But this wasn't our first rodeo. We'd interrogated intransigent subjects in the past and knew our best approach was to keep at it. We might not always obtain the full story, but we usually got more than they ever intended to share.

"Did he and the other man, Drysdale, complain between the two of them?" I asked.

"How would I know?" Her voice rose. Had we hit a nerve?

"Word hasn't gotten back to you?" Herc asked. "I thought you were in charge here. How can you manage effectively if you don't know what your most valuable resources are thinking?"

"I beg your pardon? You have no right to tell me how to run my business."

Herc straightened his shoulders. "I'm not doing that, Mrs. Sheldon. Merely commenting. You know something you've been doing your best to keep from us up to now. But our patience is running out. Time to come clean."

She backed up in her chair. "How dare you!"

Herc and I stood firm but didn't say anything further. It was her turn.

"Is that how you interview private citizens? Insult them?"

"Most private citizens go out of their way to help us. Not so much with you. We'll give you thirty seconds to start talking. After that, you'll be our guest at police headquarters."

She folded her arms across her chest and attempted to stare us down.

We waited.

"Oh, all right," she said, almost spitting it out. "I doubt it will help your case any, but since you've threatened me, I don't have much choice."

"Go on," Herc said.

"Jed felt he wasn't getting enough modeling jobs. That Trey was not only getting more than him but also getting the best ones. He had words with Trey more than once. He and Joel cornered Trey one night last week when Bart and I were gone. I only know because Lola overheard them. Trey apparently wasn't backing down and said something like they were just jealous because he had the 'it' quality that they lacked. In fact, he suggested they quit the program because they were going nowhere."

"Did you confront them?" Herc asked.

"I thought it best they work it out amongst themselves."

Sure she did. She'd stoked that fire and then backed down when the flames erupted.

"Anything more?" Herc asked.

"They fought, Trey and Jed. Joel backed off, I guess."

"Was anyone hurt?"

"Trey's face took a beating. He had to pass up a couple of jobs. Jed took one and Joel took the other. Trey was not happy." She stopped. "That's all I've got to say. The rest you'll have to learn from them, Trey and Joel, anyhow."

And now we had a motive. Persistence did occasionally pay off in this job. She hadn't wanted us to know about her battling talent. With what appeared to be the precarious state of her business, she couldn't afford to lose another model.

CHAPTER 7

"Before we talk with the two men, we'd like to get a better idea of the layout here," I said. "Starting with the fitness room, where you found him."

"Now?" Helena Sheldon was back to uncooperative mode. "I have this report to finish."

"Who knows the place better than you?" I said.

Another huff of exasperation, but she did rise. "Follow me."

How could we refuse such hospitality?

Her office was located at the end of the hallway. She opened each door along the way back to the lobby. "This is the meeting room. It also serves as the training room, which is why we leave the runway permanently set up."

Off to one side of the ten-foot runway, several chairs were arranged in a semicircle that faced a dais where a lectern took precedence.

The room across the hall appeared to be a staging area of sorts, judging by the dressing tables on one side, each weighed down with various cosmetics and creams, a giant mirror along the middle and two empty clothing racks on the other side.

She hurried on to the room next to the meeting room, a classroom of sorts. Three tables were set in an *L* shape with nine chairs around them. They faced another lectern with a white board behind it. Nine chairs? Pretty optimistic.

We passed through the lobby. She pointed to a door just off to the side. "The pool is out there."

She pulled up around the other side of what appeared to be ground floor private quarters. "This is it," she announced, throwing wide the door to the fitness room.

We stepped into this one to get a closer look. Though the room was small, Sheldon and her husband hadn't spared money to set it up. A floor-to-ceiling mirror ran along one wall, a constant reminder of the condition of the models' bodies. Hand weights filled one corner. Two treadmills, an elliptical and a stationary bike lined one wall. Arm strength machines comprised the remainder of the room.

"Would you show us where you were standing when you checked on Craddock?"

She stared at me like I'd asked her to drop through the floor. "Really?"

I nodded my head.

She took two steps forward and planted herself about ten inches to the right of the machine. "Here." Her right hand was a couple of inches from the handlebar.

"And now demonstrate the position of his body when you found him."

She made a face. "Must I?"

"I can't make you, if the memory is too much, but I'd like to get a clear image in my head of how you found him."

She shook her shoulders like a dog would shed water, then she flung a leg over the seat tube. After delicately positioning her bottom on the seat, she leaned forward and placed her head on the display console.

"Where were his hands and arms?" I asked.

She twisted her head my direction. "Surely they took photos of all this?"

"Yes, and I'll refer to them later. But rather than take the time to pull them up on my computer right now, I'd like to picture the scene."

"Hanging down at his sides," she replied grudgingly.

"And the snake? Where was it?" Herc asked, joining me in this reconstruction of the murder scene.

"On the floor. Behind him," she responded, lifting her head.

"More specific," Herc said.

She scrubbed her hands along her cheeks. "I'm not sure. Believe it or not, I was so shocked to find him most likely dead that I didn't notice it at first. I stepped back, called emergency services and then called out to everyone here. The last part was more a scream. Only then, as I attempted to resume normal breathing, did I see the thing. Like I told you before, I didn't know what it was other than it shouldn't have been in here."

She pointed to a spot about two feet behind the bike. "Afterwards, as I repeatedly replayed the scene in my head, I recalled seeing bits of something along one part of the coil. To my horror, I realized it must've been blood or tissue." She shivered. "Such a terrible way to die."

"Did you notice anything else?" I asked.

"Wasn't that *thing* enough?"

"Perhaps a scrap of fabric or clothing? Even a string or a button?"

She shook her head. "No, nothing more."

"What about smells?" Herc asked. "I'm picking up a whiff of something now." He made a show of sniffing. "What is that? Lemon?"

"Lemongrass. Joel reeks of it."

"I thought you said this room was temporarily off limits?" I said.

"It is," she replied. "He thinks it's cool to leave a lasting impression. I can't seem to convince him that impression may not be working for him."

"Did you smell it the night you found Craddock?"

"Probably. I hardly notice it anymore. It's become like white noise."

"What about the others, Compton or your husband?" I asked. "Do they wear telltale scents as well?"

"Bart prefers the woodsy stuff, but he doesn't apply it as heavily as Joel. And Trey gets complimentary men's fragrances from his shoots and uses whatever he sees first. I wear Versace, in case you wanted to know. Why do you want to know?"

"Smells are like fingerprints, only less easy to record," I told her, "because they're fleeting. Even this lemongrass odor will dissipate if we have to keep this room closed much longer. That's one of the things we're here to check out now, although all my nose is picking up is lemongrass."

"That's doesn't mean Joel's your killer. He's just been here a lot lately. You've already got your killer, which, other than seeing where she did it, is all you need to know about this place."

Herc glanced up from examining the handlebars. "That may be your opinion, Mrs. Sheldon, but we haven't made an official decision yet."

"Then unless you have something else to see while you're here, this visit is over. I have to get back to my work," she said, barely holding her anger in check.

"Please feel free to return to your office, but we still plan to talk to the other residents here. Everyone," Herc said.

She was already on her way to the door, but Herc's statement caused her to stop and turn around. "What? I told you everything there is to know."

Herc gave her a tolerant smile. "Everything we've been able to shake from you. But like we told you earlier, the plan is to interview everyone who lives here. Finish your report. We'll find our way around."

She stood there a few seconds, like she was debating whether to protest. Finally, she pivoted and left.

"Such a scintillating personality," I said to Herc as soon as we were alone.

"She knows much more than she was willing to part with," Herc replied.

"She doesn't know who our murderer is, but she suspects it's someone here. I'm pretty sure that's why she's been giving us her version of the mother hen routine."

"You don't think she did it?" he asked.

"It wouldn't have been a smart move for her, and from all we've observed, she's very much into doing what's in her best interest. Now she's down one-third of her investment. Unless she was that anxious to get rid of him, which we still need to determine, she might have clipped his wings somehow, but she wouldn't have cut short his career."

He gazed about the room. "Are we done in here?"

"I didn't have time to review the notes of the first officers on the scene. Do you know offhand if they found any physical evidence in here other than the snake?"

He shook his head. "Nothing."

If there was nothing more to see here, time to move on. "Time to check out his personal quarters," I said.

We returned to the lobby, where the daughter, Lola, had returned to her magazine at the front desk. "Trey's probably in his room," she replied when we asked. "Everyone took refuge away from the main area when they heard the police were on the property."

"You didn't," I said.

"Me? Surely you don't want to talk to me? I'm a nobody around here. Haven't you noticed? I don't have a Y chromosome."

That told us volumes. "Don't be so sure you're a nobody, Ms. Sheldon. You may have the one piece of information we're seeking, but first we want to see the victim's room."

"My last name's Benson," she replied. "I'm from my mom's first marriage. Sure, I'll stick around. All three guys have, had, rooms on the second floor. Jed was in the second. Trey's in the first room and Joel's in the third. The stairs and elevator are off to your right."

We turned to leave. "Wait," she called. "It's probably locked. The guys didn't have an open door policy with each other or any of the rest of us." She retrieved what must've been a key from a desk drawer and then opened something behind the desk we couldn't see. "Here. This is a duplicate key to his room. Just return it once you're done viewing his quarters."

We thanked her and took the stairs. Probably not Herc's preference, but one flight was good exercise for us both, and he didn't object.

The second-floor rooms all faced a walkway. A planter, filled with red geraniums, probably a holdover from the days of this being an active motel, rested on a wrought-iron stand to the side of every other room.

We went first to Craddock's space. The Benson girl had been right. It was locked. But no crime scene tape across the door, which I pointed out to Herc.

"I'll call the station and have some put up. The crime scene team apparently didn't judge his room part of the crime scene. I'll have them take photos too, so don't move anything," he told me unnecessarily.

The room included a bed, clothes closet, en suite bathroom, a small sitting area with a sofa and one chair off to one side and a tiny kitchenette off to the other. I don't know what I expected to find, other than perhaps to gain some clue as to what frame of mind Craddock had been in before heading to the fitness room.

Some clothes were laid out on his bed, but everything else seemed to be in order. Not that he was a neat freak. The bed cover had just been thrown over the bed; a couple dirty dishes, a half-finished bottle of beer and an open bag of chips rested on the tiny kitchen counter; and a men's fitness magazine lay open on the sofa.

I pointed to the snacks. "Does it seem ironic to you that he'd been drinking alcohol and snacking just prior to working out?"

He snorted. "Guys that age think they can cheat their bodies. They have no idea how time will eventually catch up with them.

Those don't tell us much about Craddock except that he wasn't a total fitness nut."

"Why had he gone to the fitness room so close to when he had to be at that meeting?" I asked.

"Again," Herc replied, "he thought he could cheat the clock. Get in his workout, take a quick shower, dress and get there on time."

I glanced at the bed again. "You're probably right. That's why that shirt, pants and underwear are on the bed. But even if he thought he could get that all in before the meeting, it still doesn't explain why he was working out at that time." The words were no sooner out than a thought occurred. "Maybe breaking up with Harper was affecting him pretty hard and he went there to blow off some steam."

"You're reading a lot into his being there at that time, although I agree, it does seem strange."

We spent the next few minutes opening drawers and going through his closet. There was no evidence he expected to be killed soon, like a will. His wastebasket was empty except for a photo of him with Harper. I pulled it up with a pair of tweezers and studied it.

"Looks like what Wickersham told us was right," Herc said. "He threw away her photo. He was done with her."

"Maybe," I replied, continuing to eye the photo. "But if he was really serious about ending things, wouldn't he have ripped it in half?"

Herc raised a brow. "Not that touchy-feely stuff already? Guys aren't as dramatic as you women. That story had ended, so he merely got rid of the evidence. That's all there was to it."

Maybe. There was no denying he'd thrown it away. But only recently, or there would've been other trash in the receptacle. Unlike Herc, I couldn't dismiss the fact it was still in one piece.

Since there didn't appear to be more to see, we left, locking the door behind us.

WE HAD TO KNOCK TWICE BEFORE COMPTON OPENED THE DOOR. "Sorry, I, uh, was wearing my earbuds."

Herc handled the intros. "Can we come in?"

"Uh, sure. If you can stand the mess. I'm not much of a house-keeper." He shot a glance around the room. Except for the remaining pink and purple bruises on his face, Trey Compton was exactly how I pictured a male model: over six feet, rich brown hair streaked with blond, brooding dark eyes and a very healthy physique.

Herc shifted aside several fashion photos that littered his small sofa, and we took our seats.

"I didn't kill Craddock, if that's what you're here for," were Compton's first words.

"We already have that in the statement you gave our officers the night we found the victim," Herc said, refusing to address the man's claim further. "We're here to clarify a few details and get your take on what happened."

"Can't help you there. I was in the meeting room waiting to get started."

"Okay, let's start there. When did you arrive at the meeting room?"

He scratched his head. "I'm not sure. A few minutes before we were supposed to start, I guess."

Herc continued to pursue this topic. "Who else was in the room when you arrived?"

Compton blinked, like he wasn't expecting the question. "Bart. And Joel. Helena came in a minute or so later."

"What about Ms. Benson?" I asked.

"Lola? She never sits in."

"Oh? Why is that? Isn't she part of the business?"

He shrugged. "Not really. She just hangs around here because she hasn't got another job."

Interesting. She was the only one who appeared to be working since we got here. Okay, not exactly working with her face in that fashion magazine, but she did appear to be staffing the front desk.

"When was the last time you used the fitness room?" Herc asked.

Compton did a quick self-check of his body. "Why? Am I looking a bit doughy?"

"That was not a comment about your appearance. I wanted to know how close in time you might've been to witnessing the murder."

"I've been nowhere near that room."

Herc didn't drop the topic. "When were you last there, Mr. Compton?"

"That morning. Around ten." Had they all taken a pledge to say as few words as possible?

"Thank you. What did you do once Mrs. Sheldon discovered the body?"

"All three of us went charging down to the room as soon as we heard her scream."

"And? What did you do next?" I asked.

"Wasn't much we could do. Craddock was dead."

"You all just stood around?"

He shrugged. "More or less. Helena had already called 9-1-1. Bart led her to a chair because she was freaking out."

"Freaking out? Explain," Herc said.

"She was upset, of course. We all were. How often do you come across a dead body? And she kept saying things like how the business would suffer. If he was going to get himself killed, why couldn't it have been somewhere else?"

Time to change the subject. "Tell us about your relationship with Craddock. Did you get on with him?" I asked.

He considered his reply. "I never planned to be a model. I was happy enough bartending. Helena's the one who came after me with tales of wealth and prestige. She never mentioned having to compete for jobs with two others. Jobs that weren't anywhere near as plentiful as she described. Craddock and I might've been good friends under other circumstances, but not when there was so much competition."

"In other words, you weren't friends," I said, interrupting him.

"If you haven't discovered this already, you will. Helena isn't a fair employer. She has her favorites. Me. For a while, I've told myself the extra attention she gave me was because I was that good. I didn't do anything to change her mind because I needed the work. Craddock and Drysdale resented the attention I was getting. Craddock more so. Most recently, he convinced Drysdale to help him rearrange my face so I wouldn't be able to take any jobs for a while."

"That pinkish-purple tinge on your face is what remains of that scuffle?" I asked, although we'd already heard about this fight from Helena Sheldon.

"Yeah. My so-called mentor informed me since I wouldn't be bringing in any money for a while, I'd have to pony up rent. I hated the idea of tending bar again, especially the way I looked. That's when she suggested an *alternative*. Apparently old Bart wasn't satisfying her needs."

Why was I not surprised by either Bart Sheldon's lack of marital prowess or Helena Sheldon seeking sexual gratification elsewhere?

Herc took it from there. "What did you decide?"

Compton hung his head. He didn't answer for several beats. "I hate myself, but I just couldn't go back and admit the modeling wasn't working out."

"Besides getting beaten up, you also have found yourself playing boy toy," I said. "Seems like the perfect storm for murder."

He took a step back and shook his head ferociously. "No! You've got to believe me. Yeah, I was planning some sort of revenge on both guys, but I hadn't acted yet. And murder was never a possibility."

"I don't know, Compton," Herc told him. "If servicing the lady was that distasteful, seems like your anger could've gotten out of control."

"The topic of the meeting we were supposed to have was a change to the compensation plan. I decided to hold off doing anything until I heard what the Sheldons had in mind. Like I said, we weren't getting the jobs we'd been promised. I suspected they were about to lay off one or two of us. Maybe even close down entirely. I didn't want to do anything that would hurt my chances of staying on."

"Any idea what will happen now that Craddock is no longer around?" I asked.

"Depends on how much bad publicity his death brings. If his girlfriend killed him, since the plumber's tool was the murder weapon, we should be able to regain whatever reputation we had." A new thought occurred to him. "Why are you still investigating? You've got the culprit. As soon as you put her away, the rest of us can get back to normal."

We didn't usually reply to such questions, and we didn't now.

"What's the name of the bar where you used to work?" Herc asked.

"Why do you need that?"

What was it about the residents of this place? So far, they challenged us question after question.

"Background check purposes, Mr. Compton," Herc told him.

"They have little good to say about me these days. They've accused me of acting like I'm better than them."

"We'll keep that in mind," Herc said.

Compton reluctantly gave us the name of the bar. At this point, that might not be necessary, but we had it in case we needed it.

We thanked him and went to find Lola Benson again, hoping she could tell us where to find Bart Sheldon and Joel Drysdale.

CHAPTER 8

We caught up with Bart Sheldon at a table next to the pool, reading the newspaper.

"I prefer the old-fashioned way to get my news," he said after we introduced ourselves.

My first impression of him was that of an aging movie star attempting to look twenty years younger with his thick head of abnormally black hair, too-tight black tee and aviator sunglasses. He set aside his glass of whatever liquid. "I take it you want to ask me about Craddock, which is easy. I hardly knew him."

"Really? We were told you are a full participant in the business," Herc said.

Sheldon settled back and folded his hands together across his stomach. "The business end. Helena is the big-idea person, but she falls apart when it comes to reading budget sheets."

"What about training sessions?" I asked. "Didn't you lead some of them?"

"Lead? Good one. Helena was indisposed a few times—read that 'hung over'—so I stood in for her. Made up lessons on the spot." He chuckled.

"There were only three students," I said. "Surely you noticed Jed Craddock then?"

"Was he the blond? Less attractive than the other two, if you ask me. But as far as any conversations I might've had with him, can't help you there."

"Tell us about what happened when you discovered his body," Herc asked, moving on to what would hopefully be something the man knew more about.

"I followed the two models, more out of curiosity than concern. Helena was already on the phone calling for an ambulance. The two guys both examined the body. When it was clear nothing could be done for him, one of them, the one with the blond streaks, went to comfort Helena and the other went outside, I assume to wait for the first responders."

"And you, Mr. Sheldon?" I asked.

"Me? Someone had to take control. Helena certainly wasn't up to it, and the two men just stood around like they had no idea what was going on."

"Did you notice anything unusual about the room?"

"Except for Craddock, it was empty, because Helena's meeting was about to start. Usually pretty crowded that time of day. Those guys are fanatics when it comes to their bodies. Helena is constantly on their case about staying in shape. I've even tried to use the equipment myself on occasion, but there's always been someone else there."

"Can you account for your whereabouts before you went to the meeting?" Herc asked.

"I was here. In our suite. Watching the news."

"Did anyone see you?"

"Helena came in about a half hour before it was to start to change clothes. Wanted to wear one of her power suits, since she anticipated the topic wouldn't go over well."

"What exactly were you going to tell your people at this meeting we keep hearing about?" I asked.

He picked up his glass again. "Better ask Helena about that. Helena's in charge of staff relations."

"Just give us the bottom line, since we're not staff."

"You've probably gathered from the looks of things around here that we're not exactly bringing in the bucks. The meeting was to announce how we planned to deal with it."

Herc cut to the chase. "Are you shutting down?"

Sheldon shook his head. "No, no, nothing quite so drastic. You'll have to get the details from Helena."

He reopened his paper, dismissing us. We don't usually let the interviewee decide when to terminate an interview, but we'd already realized we weren't getting much more from this guy anyhow.

We left Sheldon with his paper and returned to the lobby. Lola was nowhere to be seen, so it was just the two of us conferring. "Three down, two to go," I said. "I assume you want to hit everyone today?"

"Yeah, we can pick through what we've learned over a late lunch, but let's finish this first go now."

"You're still here?" Lola Benson said, reappearing at the desk.

"A little longer," I replied. "We'd like to speak with Joel Drysdale next, if he's here?"

"Oh, sure. His room is number three upstairs."

We made our way back to the second-floor rooms, passing Compton's as we went.

Drysdale was about the same height as Compton but somewhat leaner. Perhaps a runner? The greenest eyes I'd ever seen gazed back at us in greeting, augmented by the pale green golf shirt he wore. And there was no way not to note the distinct scent of lemongrass.

"Word has spread that you're here," Drysdale said when he came to his door. "Gave me a chance to clean up." He pointed to a small sectional. "Have a seat. I take it you want to know where I was just before we found poor Jed in the fitness room. I watch a lot of crime shows on TV."

"Okay, we'll start there," I said, "and return to some background information about you afterwards. So, where were you just before the victim was discovered?"

"Helena called this special meeting for seven that night. It was a last-minute thing. I didn't get notice until two in the afternoon. I suspected whatever she planned to say wouldn't be good. Things around here haven't been good in weeks. My guess was that one or more of us was about to be out on the streets unemployed. Although I wasn't looking forward to it, I got there early at six fifty, the first to arrive. Trey came next, then Bart. Helena showed up a minute or two later."

"Was Craddock typically late?"

"No. He and I both felt ourselves under the gun in recent weeks. What few jobs came in went to Compton. Neither of us had done anything to irritate Helena. We thought Compton had a little side action going with her. Anyway, we'd both been doing everything in our power to stay on her good side, which included promptness."

"Did you think it odd that Craddock wasn't there?" Herc asked.

"Not at first, but once Helena arrived and discovered he hadn't shown yet, she asked us all more than once where he was. She's not a very patient woman. Meetings start on her time, not others'. She checked her watch more than once, then started pacing. I'm pretty sure she was anxious to deliver whatever bad news she had to tell and get out of there. She hadn't planned on the delay."

"Did you all go to search for him?" Herc asked next.

"Can't say for sure. I was the first out the door. I went directly to his room. The door was locked, so I called for him more than once. Now I know why there was no answer. I don't know if Compton or Sheldon joined the search or not. Lola wasn't at the meeting and was nowhere to be seen when I went up to the second-floor rooms. There are some vacant rooms on the second floor. When I didn't hear from Craddock, I went to check them. I was on the second one when I heard Helena's scream."

"Did you go directly to the fitness room?" I asked.

"I wasn't sure where the scream came from except that it had come from the first floor, so I headed downstairs. I followed Helena's screams. By the time I arrived, her hollering had turned to a rant. Compton attempted to get the body off the bike and down on the floor where we could try CPR. I helped him. Bart must've arrived after us."

"But before the first responders?" I continued.

"Yeah. By the time the professionals got there, we'd done our best to revive him, but we could tell from the start it was a losing cause."

I didn't recall Compton having mentioned that he and Drysdale had removed Craddock from the bike to revive him. "Where did the body wind up on the floor in relation to the bike?" I asked.

He narrowed his eyes as if picturing the scene again. "Compton lifted him up under his arms from the right side. I stood on the same side on the front of the bike and hefted up his legs. So his body stretched on the floor from just in front of the handlebar to several feet past the back of the bike. You should have photos because that's where his body remained until it was taken away."

"Yes, we do," I replied, "but we wanted to verify the location with you. Where did you and the other three stand?"

"I let Compton do the CPR thing, so I was in front of the bike at first, and when Craddock couldn't be revived, I moved around the front of the bike and lighted in the back to leave room for the EMTs when they got there. Compton remained bent over the body's right side and didn't move from there, like he couldn't believe the guy wasn't breathing. Helena wasn't much good after calling 9-1-1. Bart got her into a chair, where she continued to wring her hands and moan about the future of the studio. I don't know what Bart did after that. Must've stayed near the back."

This description finished, he settled a hip against a desk across the room from us.

"Thank you," Herc said. "That fills in a few points about the murder scene. Now we'd like to know a little more about you. What's your background, and how did you wind up here?"

"A few years back, I worked for a modeling agency in Miami. Did pretty well there, but being part of a large stable and getting my assignments from someone else didn't work for me. After four years of that grind, I decided to go out on my own. Helena saw me at one of the shows I did during that period and asked me to join the new agency she was forming here in Shasta. Given my previous experience, she asked me to also serve as trainer for the other models she planned to hire.

"As it turned out, I only do a little of the training. Helena and Bart do the lion's share. We have mini-lectures daily and are expected to put an hour in at the pool and two in the fitness room. We each have a weekly makeup session with Helena. Craddock told me more than once he suspected that routine was imposed simply to keep us occupied so we don't figure out nothing else of importance is happening in our careers. Lately, jobs have even slowed down for Trey."

"Any idea why that has been the case?" I asked. We'd been so focused on the details of the case and the key suspects, we hadn't really paid much attention to the state of the agency, which was turning out to be an underlying motive.

"This is purely observation on my part, but this business is built on relationships. There are a gazillion great-looking men and women out there, all capable of showing off clients' products. Those who need models require guidance finding just the right ones, *guidance* which boils down to someone they trust suggesting a name. That's where either the head of the agency or someone specifically charged with marketing comes in. Helena likes to think that's her. Unfortunately, well—you've met her. Public relations isn't her strong suit."

That explained a lot. Up to a point. "But she appears to be a savvy businesswoman. Surely she's realized by now she's getting in her own way?" I asked.

"You'd think so, wouldn't you?" Drysdale replied. "But I've learned she's pretty much a one-trick pony. Even if she has figured out she's the source of her problems, I don't know if she's smart enough to find another way."

"What about her husband?" Herc asked, uncharacteristically drawn into this business strategy discussion.

"Bart Sheldon actually do some work? Nah, the guy's here for a free ride. Craddock's death could be a signal of other changes to come."

"What did he do before he married Mrs. Sheldon?" I asked. I made a mental note to check further on that. Thus far, the guy hadn't been very forthcoming with us.

"No idea, although I've seen him herding a couple shady-looking characters from the building a couple times. I don't know if they were just old friends or if he'd worked with them in the past."

"Shady as in crooked?" Herc asked.

"Maybe. I wouldn't be surprised. The guy's a real tool. Jed mentioned something a while back, but I was preoccupied at the time, and the subject never came up again."

Herc and I exchanged looks. Another point to check out later.

"How did you get along with Craddock?" I asked.

"Okay, I guess. We started out friendly enough with each other, but competition for jobs can do strange things to a person. You find yourself questioning whatever they say, wondering if it's a setup to get you to leave. The three of us pretty much kept to ourselves the last few weeks unless we had to be in training together."

"And the others," I continued, "how do you get along with them?"

"Helena and Bart? I had to stay on their good side just to keep my job. I did that best keeping my distance."

"Must be pretty lonely," I said.

"It's not that bad. Got my TV and books. And there's always Lola, when she's not hiding from her mother."

Was that why we hadn't seen her much when we'd been in the lobby? "Why's that?" Herc asked.

Drysdale stared at Herc. "That's the woman we've just been talking about. Surely you know what I mean?"

"I get what you mean as far as your relationship with Mrs. Sheldon goes, but what have you noticed between her and her daughter?"

Drysdale changed position. "You've met Lola, I take it? Gorgeous. Strange why her mother hasn't tried to get her into modeling. Friendly, too, which may be the cause of the problem. Helena doesn't like her talking to the three of us, like what's she supposed to do? There's rarely anyone else around."

Lola Benson. The only person here we had yet to interview. She apparently was the only one who hadn't been present when Craddock's body was found, but she might still know more about what happened to him than the others were letting on. Time to find out.

CHAPTER 9

We thanked Drysdale for his input and asked where he thought we might find the young Benson woman if she wasn't at the front desk. He suggested we try the Sheldon living quarters.

Since she wasn't at the desk, we followed what Drysdale had suggested and went to the family's private apartment. We had to knock a few times before she answered the door. "Sorry. I was in back in my mini-suite and didn't hear you at first," she said, inviting us in.

"We've talked to everyone except you," Herc said by way of opening.

"I'm glad you decided I might have something to add," she said. "Although as little as they tell me about things around here, I'm not sure what that might be."

I didn't address that comment. "Let's start with some general background, Ms. Benson. Tell us about yourself. What is your job with the agency?"

"I've only lived here with my mom during the last year. I was at college up in Gainesville before that, studying biology. I'd been living with a guy I met my freshman year. My time with him tanked about the same time my grades dipped. I couldn't say which caused the other. It all came at me at once, enough for me to drop out. I didn't want to come here, but it seemed the best path to take while I got my head straight again."

"And your mom gave you a job here?" Herc asked.

"That was Bart's idea. In exchange for room and board. You've probably noticed how the agency is pretty much limping along on its last leg. I chose to work here to relieve my mother of paying for an assistant. I do all the administrative tasks she doesn't want to do, which is most of them. I keep irregular hours at the desk. No real need to be there constantly. There's no walk-in traffic. Occasionally someone will book an appointment with Mother to discuss a modeling job. I'm there at the desk to greet them to make it look like we're an active business." Which explained why she hadn't been at the desk on a few of the times when we'd gone through the lobby.

"How well did you know Jed Craddock?" Herc asked.

She tipped her head to the side slightly. "Per my mother, I'm not supposed to mix with the talent."

"Oh? Why is that?" I was interrupting Herc, but my curiosity got the better of me.

She glanced away before replying. "I'm not sure. She never said. If I had to guess, I'd say it was because she didn't want me distracting them. Paying more attention to one than another. Things like that. Once or twice, she's hinted that the less interaction these guys had with any female, the more testosterone in their systems for their work."

Interesting theory. Did Helena really believe it or was she just attempting to avoid dissention amongst the troops? I couldn't resist a follow-up. "And did you avoid mixing with the men?"

She studied her hands. "Do I have to answer that?"

"It could be pertinent to the case."

She released a long breath. "It gets boring at the desk, even though I'm not there all that much. Not much more lively back in my suite. So maybe on occasion I chat things up with one of them."

"Any one in particular?" Herc asked, also becoming interested.

"Um, Jed."

"Recently?"

She appeared to consider. "A month ago?"

"More than once?"

"Maybe twice? Or three times?"

"Just casual conversation?"

She bit a lip. "Um, at first. But one time we got to talking and joking, and one thing led to another, and before I knew it, he was in my bed."

"Does anyone else know about your time with him?"

One hand went to the bracelet on her other hand and began twiddling it.

"Ms. Benson?" I asked.

"Trey." It came out in a very tiny voice.

"How did he react to the news?" Herc asked.

She pursed her lips. She had to know we'd have a follow-up question, but she acted like she wasn't expecting us to get so personal. "I don't know for sure, but I could hear them arguing upstairs somewhere."

Herc continued. "Was he jealous?"

"I, uh, guess. I sorta had also been seeing Trey before Jed and I got together."

All that earlier talk about being told to stay away from the guys obviously hadn't been heeded. Which brought up another question. "What about Joel Drysdale?" I asked. "Have you been with him also?"

She played some more with her bracelet and deliberately didn't look at us.

I pressed. "Is that a yes?"

"You've gotta understand." Her voice was a whine. "After my boyfriend and I broke up, I felt like my world had ended. I was even more sure of that when I came here and had to see my mom cuddling up to that smarmy Bart Sheldon every day." Now she did look at us. "I'm not a slut, even though it sorta came out that way. I've been terribly lonely and bored. The guys relieved some of that. I thought I'd been so careful keeping each from knowing I was seeing the other two. I did pretty well, too, until Bart walked in on Jed and me."

"Your stepfather knew also?" I couldn't keep my voice from rising.

"Didn't I say that? I thought my room was off-limits to him and my mother. After all, I'm twenty, almost twenty-one. He claimed afterwards, after he literally threw Jed out of my suite, that he thought he heard my cries for help. No way! I decided then and there, even before Jed was, you know, that I'm getting out of here as soon as I can."

This was the first we'd heard about any problems between Sheldon and Craddock. Time to zero in.

"When did this happen?" I asked.

"I don't know. Maybe two weeks ago? That's about when Trey found out about us."

"What did your stepfather do after he chased Mr. Craddock from your room?" I asked.

"He went straight to my mom. Within an hour, she was in my room reminding me I wasn't to socialize with the guys. She told me if this happened again, I'd be looking for a new place to live. That was after a lot of hand-wringing and tears, telling me how ungrateful I was that she'd come to my rescue after I did so poorly in school."

"Would it be safe to say your relationship with your mother and Sheldon has gone downhill since then?" I asked.

"How does that relate to Jed's murder?" she asked.

"Just answer her question, Ms. Benson," Herc said.

"My mom and I haven't gotten along in some time. Before I went away to school, I didn't like the idea of her marrying Bart Sheldon and told her so repeatedly. Allowing me to live and work here was about as far as her motherly love would stretch. Ever since I was a teen, she's been jealous of me. Owning a modeling agency where looks are supreme has only made my presence here more difficult."

"What about Sheldon?" Herc asked. "How's he treated you?"

"Did he ever hit on me? No, but I suspect only because my mother made sure she was always around to head that off. Not to protect me though. She didn't want me to take him away from her."

"But you still don't like him, right?"

"No. I've never disguised my feelings about the man. He's a creep."

"In what way?" I asked. "Has he ever done anything to you directly to make you feel that way?"

"When I was younger, before I went away to school and before they owned this place, he'd pop into my room uninvited with a variety of reasons for checking on me. My mother had a fit when I started locking my door. After the first few times of telling her about his 'visits' and being told I was imagining things, I stopped complaining and stayed on alert. I bought a ball bat and stuck it under my bed. Since I've been back, I've insisted my doors be locked."

"Anything else?" Herc asked.

"He doesn't do much work around here, as much as he claims he's the business head. That was no surprise, because I always thought he was lazy and living off my mother. He disappears for hours at a time. She always explains it away as his needing his space or going off for runs, but he's got plenty of space around here plus a fitness room. Not too long ago, I saw him out in the parking lot talking to a guy who looked even smarmier than him. I couldn't hear what they were saying, but from their gestures, they weren't exactly friends."

"When did you see him with that guy?" I asked.

She took a moment to think about it. "A few weeks back. I don't remember an exact date, and I couldn't describe the guy other than he had long, dark hair and a beard."

"You said they didn't look friendly. Were they arguing? Did they exchange blows?"

She shook her head. "No, they didn't come to blows, although the other guy stood close to Sheldon and shook his first at him."

"Did you confront Sheldon about what you observed?" Herc asked.

"Bart Sheldon isn't the kind of person you challenge. Not that he would out-argue you. No, instead, he's so oily, he never answers a question directly. He just talks around the subject. I didn't say anything to him or anyone else about what I witnessed, but I kept a closer watch on him after that. I didn't see him with that guy or anyone else again, but a couple times he went outside to make phone calls."

I eyed Herc. We seemed to have come to the end of the road with her. "Anything else you noticed about the three models?" Herc asked.

"Ever since Sheldon found Jed in my room, all three guys have avoided me. Guess I should've expected as much. But they've also avoided each other. They used to mess around on the basketball court or in the swimming pool. Not anymore."

"Thank you for sharing your observations with us," I told her.

Herc gave her his card. "Call me if anything else occurs to you."

She quickly tucked it away in the pocket of her shorts.

"Okay," she replied. "Are you done here?"

"For now," Herc answered. "We need to gather our notes from today's interviews, consider what we've learned and identify any holes. We may be back."

"Don't wait long. I think Mom might be closing this place down soon, especially now that she only has two models."

"We'll keep that in mind," I said as Herc and I made our way toward her door.

CHAPTER 10

"My head is throbbing," I said as we climbed into Herc's car.

"Par for the course, Ro," he replied, attempting to sound blasé. He was probably being bombarded with as many divergent opinions as I, but he was trying to be the cool one.

"Time for a very late lunch." I felt like I could devour a full smorgasbord, but by the time I actually ordered, I settled for a barbecued beef sandwich.

"How much stock would you place on what the daughter told us?" Herc asked in between bites of his meatball hoagie.

"She could be a pathological liar, which would negate everything she told us," I said. "But my better judgment is telling me she was on the up and up."

"Which means the others were either lying or left out quite a few details pertinent to the case."

"Now we spend the rest of the day sorting out what we've learned and separating truth from fiction," I returned.

"My gut tells me it will take longer than today. But first, let's get back to our improvised murder board and list the facts we do know."

The Shasta police department was fairly advanced technologically, so at some point after we'd worked through our initial thought process, we'd need to enter our findings in the department's database. But for now, to simplify our thinking, we'd go first to the two whiteboards I kept at my place.

Since we'd just eaten, we skipped our usual snacks once we reached my duplex, although we both had a glass of water.

"Let's just throw out our ideas as they occur to us," Herc said.

"I'll try to put our thoughts in some kind of order on the whiteboard," I replied.

1. *Jed Craddock strangled with plumber's snake*
2. *Snake belonged to Harper Wickersham, his former girlfriend with whom he just broke up*
3. *Wickersham denies being near the studio at time of death and has an alibi for estimated time of death; visited there on occasion before breakup*
4. *Craddock alone in fitness room*
5. *Body found on exercise bike in fitness room by Helena Sheldon just after 7 p.m.*
6. *Compton next in room, then Drysdale, finally Bart Sheldon*
7. *Snake on floor on right behind bike*
8. *Helena Sheldon called EMS*
9. *Sheldon Studio appears to be in financial trouble; Craddock killed prior to meeting where layoffs might have been announced (they called it a change in compensation plan)*
10. *Trey Compton favored over the other two men; they confronted him a few weeks ago and Craddock beat him up*
11. *Craddock caught in bed with Helena Sheldon's daughter a few weeks ago*
12. *Compton and Drysdale also hooked up with daughter previously; Compton fought with Craddock after he learned they'd been together*
13. *Mother forbade daughter to mix it up with the men, threatened to throw her out if it happens again, although*

> *according to Compton, Helena Sheldon wasn't above*
> *suggesting sex with him*
> 14. *Sheldon supposedly disappeared from time to time*
> 15. *Sheldon seen in argument with unknown stranger a few*
> *weeks before incident*

We got that far before needing a break. "Pretty good summation," Herc said after reading through our list.

"There were so many undercurrents coming at us when we talked to everyone, we need to go back through what we learned from each of them and strip out the feelings from the facts."

"You know I only do hard evidence, Ro. That touchy-feely stuff you do may help augment our findings eventually, but we're not getting anywhere until we finalize this list."

Most of our cases, both recent and past, involved some kind of discussion like this. We came at our investigations different ways. We were a good blend. But first we had to work through this initial debriefing standoff. I'd learned to hold my feelings in check until the time was ripe.

"Okay, hard evidence it is," I said, my usual refrain. "The man was strangled with a plumber's snake, at least that's the theory until we get verification from the medical examiner. It was done from behind, although we don't know yet if the killer surprised the victim. The snake belonged to the victim's girlfriend, Harper Wickersham. He'd just broken up with her a few days before."

"Good start. Comments?"

"You've met Wickersham," I replied. "She's too smart to leave the weapon behind. I'm 95% convinced someone's trying to frame her, unless we discover other evidence against her."

"You're dismissing her as a suspect?" he asked.

"Not ruling her out but putting her low on the list. If the death was due to strangulation and if the snake was the weapon, it tells us this was planned in advance, first-degree murder. Craddock's run-ins with Compton were more of a spontaneous nature. Supposedly Compton fought with him after learning Craddock had been with Lola Benson. Since then, it appears both Craddock and Drysdale attacked Compton when they learned he was getting more jobs than them. Conceivably, Compton could've planned this murder in advance as his revenge."

"So Compton goes high on the list. What about Drysdale?"

"We don't know enough about Drysdale yet, other than he tends to go heavy on his lemongrass fragrance. According to Ms. Benson, she'd been with him, too, so it's possible he murdered Craddock out of revenge. We need to learn more about his past. Helena Sheldon said he was a former model who agreed to train the other two."

Clearly, we'd only scratched the surface with our interviews today. We needed to research the backgrounds of those persons of interest as well as talk to them again.

"That leaves the woman, Helena Sheldon, her husband, Bart, and her daughter, Lola Benson," Herc said.

"Interesting contrast there," I replied. "As well as family dynamic. Helena Sheldon told us as little as possible until you did your official thing. Don't know what to make of that. It could be she just doesn't like the police. Or she could be hiding something. That something could be what we already have learned from talking to the others: her business is in big trouble financially. Bart Sheldon didn't tell us much either, but to borrow the description used by Lola Benson, he came across as quite smarmy. Doesn't suggest much of a motive."

"And the daughter?" Herc asked.

"The most talkative. We hadn't heard much about the antagonism amongst the three models until we got to her. Could be just a clever ruse for sidetracking us. She had no problem suggesting her feelings about her mother and stepfather. She seemed to get on well with the three models, if for no other reason than to reduce her boredom."

"Not on the suspect list then?"

"She's still on there, all right. She may be young but not too young to spin a tale to divert our interest. But right now I can't think why she would've wanted to kill him."

"Could be more to that story about going to bed with Craddock," Herc said.

"Good thought, except is she strong enough to have strangled him with that snake?"

"We certainly thought Wickersham was at first. And we haven't dismissed the Sheldon woman as the strangler either," he pointed out.

"Wickersham is a plumber. She's built up the muscles to do it, even though I more or less dismissed her. And Helena Sheldon is big enough to strangle a cow."

"That covers the crew at the Sheldon Agency. Anyone else we should consider?" Herc asked.

Had he arrived at the same point I had? "Interesting you should ask. So far, no one sticks out as having a powerful enough motive to murder Craddock. More than likely, it's there somewhere, buried. However, it's possible someone else snuck onto the property and killed him. That layout is fairly open, especially since Lola Benson is rarely at the front desk. If that's the case, we have a whole new slate of suspects to find. We have to look at Craddock's life beyond the agency."

"We've got a lot on our plate tomorrow. Where do you want to start?"

"With Wickersham. Hopefully, she can shed more light on his background than she's given us thus far."

"Ennis and Dexter are on another assignment, but Janet Oliver is still available to do research work for us back at the office," Herc said. Greg Ennis and Isla Dexter were uniformed cops who'd recently helped protect my friends and me from a drug lord and his cronies. Janet Oliver, a civilian, was a top-notch administrative assistant who worked mainly for Herc unless needed elsewhere.

"Good. Can you still contact her today and get her started looking into the modeling agency?"

"I'll text her now and expand that request to the Sheldons in their pre-modeling agency days."

"Then I'll transfer these notes to the department's computerized murder board to go with the evidence already collected," I said. One of these days I had to request one of those new computerized whiteboards. For now, I was more comfortable with this process.

Our path decided, Herc made ready to leave. Now that he'd more or less accepted Chuck and me as a couple, he didn't linger and hint at having dinner with me.

Time for me to relax and wait for my deli man, as Herc called him, to return home.

CHAPTER 11

Jason had made himself scarce during my debriefing session with Herc, but that was typical. Long ago, my protective feline had decided it was every cat and human to themselves whenever Herc Morgan was around. I'd attributed his attitude to their mutual jealousy. Somehow Chuck fell into a different category; Jason at least tolerated him and stayed in the same room when Chuck was around. In fact, of late, he was allowing Chuck to touch him, especially at those times when Chuck brought him a new toy.

"Hey, guy," I called when he hadn't appeared even after Herc had been gone for several minutes. He had more hiding places in my condo than I'd ever discover, but I went looking for him nonetheless. When he hadn't shown up after a few more minutes, I headed to the cupboard where I kept his favorite treats. He most likely was watching from somewhere and would deign to appear as soon as he saw them.

But he didn't. I started calling him more persuasively. Still no Jason. I dropped to the floor and sat there, waiting for him. When I still hadn't seen him after another five minutes, I rose and called Val. "Have you been over here at all today?"

"No. Did you expect me to check in?"

"No. It's just that Jason hasn't appeared. Herc was here for a while, which is when Jason usually hides out. But Herc's been gone over fifteen minutes and still no Jason. Even when I put out his favorite treats."

"I'll be right over."

She slammed through the front door within a minute. "Would've been here sooner, but I put on a pair of shoes." She joined me at the kitchen table. "Is he upset with you like he was when you were gone several days looking for Ryder's sister?"

"Not that I'm aware. I was gone the better part of the day on this new case, but Herc and I got here around three, much earlier than my usual schedule."

"You've checked his usual haunts around the place?"

"Yes, although I only know half of them."

She rose. "Let me give it a try." Off she went, calling him lovingly as she opened closet doors, glanced behind furniture and then headed upstairs for more surveillance.

Meanwhile, I wandered aimlessly around the kitchen attempting to keep my mind active to avoid worrying. I guess I made a fresh pot of coffee, although I don't remember going through the motions. I kept returning to his food dish, wondering if he'd eaten something that made him sick. I didn't know he was sick, but the thought wouldn't go away. We'd been lucky with our boy ever since Ryder had found him and brought him to us for safekeeping. Jason had been the picture of health ever since. Val and I had religiously taken him to the vet for periodic checkups. Once in a while, we took him to a young woman who trimmed his nails.

"Okay, don't panic yet," Val said, reentering the room. "No sign of him. But I also didn't see any sign of vomit or pee, which is what the vet told us to look for if we ever thought he might be sick."

I gazed down at the mug of coffee I didn't remember pouring and set it on the table without having taken a single sip. "You didn't hear him either? No mewling?"

She shook her head.

"I guess that's a good sign?" I had no idea whether it was or not. This was new territory for us. All I knew to do was to hang in there and not lose it.

Fortunately, Chuck came through the back door about then. "Evenin' ladies. Am I interrupting something?"

Val came out of the fog first. "Not at all. We need your help. Jason is hiding. He won't come out."

He looked directly at me. "Uh, anything happen between you and our friend?"

"If he's angry with me, I have no idea," I replied. "I just wish he'd come out so we could figure out if there is something physically wrong with him."

"When was the last time you took him to the vet?" Chuck asked.

"Last month. For his annual checkup. She pronounced him in fine shape. His weight was within norms. His coat was healthy. And he actually demonstrated his better personality that day and let her examine him without showing his claws or holding back. I have no idea what's happened in the last month to change all that."

"You don't suppose he's feeling neglected again?"

"Not unless his expectations are changing," I said. "I suppose that's possible, but he's become pretty accustomed to our schedules. There's not been much change in them. He's not much for change."

Chuck poured himself a cup of the coffee I'd just made and took a sip. "There has been one change. Me."

"Oh, no. He likes you, Chuck."

"Tolerates me. Gets along with me, mainly because I bring him gifts every so often. But he no longer sleeps with you at night."

"That was his choice," I quickly pointed out. "You didn't throw him out."

"I, uh, think I'll be going," Val said, apparently ill at ease with this latest topic. "Call me when he does show up. Or if ..."

"I'm sure he'll come out sometime," I replied. "He just wants to keep us on tenterhooks." I glanced at Chuck. "He likes being in control like that."

"You don't suppose it's become a male versus male thing between the two of us?" Chuck asked after Val had left.

"I don't think so. If that were the case, he'd disappear each night when you arrive. He'd be here waiting to have me alone until then."

Chuck pursed his lips. "Maybe. But let's see how he reacts to me when he finally does show."

"When. Right." Sounded so simple. Logical. So why was my stomach so queasy?

Dinner was somewhat quieter than usual, not that Jason added that much noise when he was around, but both Chuck and I kept our voices down as we discussed the events of our day.

"I take it you've reconciled with your pal, since you're helping him with his latest case?"

"Yeah. With Al becoming the sought-after star of the department with his new forensic accounting skills, once again, Jim and Herc turned to me. A little sooner than I would've liked after our last case, but you can't schedule murder."

"Should I be worried with you now spending your time with male models?" he asked.

I had to laugh. "Not when one could be a murderer. Besides, they're both a decade younger than Val, so imagine how much younger they are than me."

"Since when has age been a problem when the lady is such a stunner?" he said, taking my hand in his.

At that beautiful sentiment, Jason made himself known.

I dove for him at once. "Hi, boy!" I said with more relief than I expected. "Where've you been?"

Jason didn't pause for his usual preening session. Instead, he moved away from both of us and headed off to his food bowls. But once he got to his dinner, he only took a few bites before moving off, padding his way toward one of his favorite spots, the end of the sofa in the living room.

"What did you make of that?" I asked Chuck.

"Not sure," he responded. "Has this happened before?"

I followed Jason as far as the door between the kitchen and dining room. "He seemed okay. At least he was breathing fine and his coat looked okay."

I texted Val that our boy had revealed himself, although he hadn't appeared too hungry. She replied, asking if I wanted her to come back. I told her it wasn't necessary unless the odd behavior got worse.

"Do you need to contact his vet?" Chuck asked.

"Not yet. Let's just watch him for now." I said it with as much confidence as I could muster, but I couldn't dismiss this feeling that all was not well with my feline roommate.

CHAPTER 12

I met Herc in the station's small conference room the next morning, picking up coffee and doughnuts on my way. We'd made good progress the day before as we'd begun our interviews, and we'd developed a considerable list of information collected, but now we needed to step back and analyze what we had and what we still needed. Clearly, we were nowhere near identifying the killer.

Herc was waiting for me. "You read my mind," he said as he eyed the goodies I'd brought.

"Unless you folks have found a new coffee maker to replace that contraption that purports to produce a decent brew, I came prepared." I handed him a container along with two packets of sugar and a tub of cream, knowing his preferences.

"I asked Janet Oliver to sit in. I guess she'll have to make do with the company joe."

"She brought her own beverage," Janet said from the door. "Hi, Mrs. Summerfield. Good to see you again." Fair-skinned with hazel eyes, Janet wore her curly blond hair cut short. I wasn't sure if that was for ease of care or to look less feminine. Probably the latter, because her outfit of choice was usually a pair of slacks, a blazer and a tailored shirt. Today the shirt was a crisp white and the pants and jacket a charcoal gray. She set a cup and thermos on the conference room table before pulling out a chair.

She was growing into her job. A few months ago, if she'd been asked to join us, she would've waited for the invitation to sit. Not that it would've been necessary then any more than it was now. In the interim, she'd been promoted from intern to a permanent job as researcher while she decided if she wanted to go on to formal law enforcement training. She'd make a good cop, but a part of me wished she'd stay on and help Herc in this capacity. But that was a foolish thought, since I kept saying each case on which I consulted for the department was my last and Herc kept hinting he was soon to retire.

"Last night, I asked Janet to start researching the finances of the Sheldon Studio as well as the backgrounds of Helena and Bart Sheldon," he told me, repeating his parting words the night before. "Did you have much time to get into that assignment?" he asked her.

"So far, I've only been able to find basic background on the two Sheldons. Their finances are even more difficult to unscramble. At least at this preliminary stage. Not to worry, though. I've got a few ideas how to dig deeper once we're finished here."

"Tell us what you've managed to gather so far," Herc said.

She brought up a screen on her device and started to read. "Helena Sheldon, forty-two, born in Naperville, Illinois. Attended Morton College in Cicero, Illinois, for part of a year. Apparently met her first husband, Merle Benson, there. He was home on leave from the naval base in Pensacola, Florida. They were married six months later and then she moved to Florida to be with him.

"Couldn't find much on her early work history. My guess is she worked off the grid for a while."

"Any evidence that might've been illegal activity?" I asked, our recent search for Ryder's sister, Melinda Horne, in mind. Melinda had worked as a paid escort in Atlanta for a few years.

She shook her head. "Not that I've found thus far. No arrests during those early years. One child, Lola Jean, born after they'd been in Florida a couple years, making her twenty now. Benson was honorably discharged from the service six months after the child was born. He worked in construction the next several years, which brought the young family to the Orlando area after a few years. I picked up some employment data on her about then. She worked in various restaurants as a dishwasher, server and cook.

"They were divorced after twelve years. Benson stayed in the area, but she headed to Miami, taking the girl with her. She did clerical work the next few years at a small TV station there. She was eventually promoted to secretary, to station manager and then manager. I found a few photos on the internet of her at dinner or some social event with various TV personalities and other entertainment types, mostly locals but in later years a few with ties to larger markets.

"She married Bart Sheldon four years ago. Benson was killed in a construction accident six months after that. He named his daughter, Lola, as his sole beneficiary, but since she was still a minor, the insurance money has been held in trust until she turns twenty-one, which is in three months. Helena Sheldon has served as trustee until that time. I still have some digging to do in their financial records, but it would appear Helena Sheldon has somehow been able to dip into that money to purchase the motel and set up her modeling studio. I suspect but still need to prove that those funds were what paid for Lola's tuition."

"If that's the case," Herc said, "Lola doesn't need to work for her room and board. She already owns the studio."

"Does Lola know that?" I asked. "That information alone gives us a whole new line of inquiry."

"There's a little more," Oliver said. "On Bart Sheldon. Fifty-three years old. Born and grew up here in central Florida. Graduated from high school in St. Cloud. A farmhand on the local ranches for several years. Got into feed sales and later farm implements in his thirties. I couldn't find a specific date when he met Helena, but there are a few photos of them on the studio's website that go back seven or eight years. One was taken four years ago with some guy who's supposed to be a famous male model, Zane Billings, which predates the opening of the agency by two years. Significant? I'll leave that to you two to figure out.

"Anyway, though he's never been arrested, he's been questioned by the police a number of times in recent years, both before and since they opened the studio. Here, in Orlando and in Miami."

"What for?" Herc asked.

"Suspicion of robbery years ago and more recently suspicion of trafficking in stolen goods. Never enough proof. The file notes speculate he and his cronies had received prior notice each time they were raided."

Very interesting. More to check into.

"Do the notes indicate what kind of goods were stolen?" I asked.

She read further. "It appears to have varied. Small things, like computer parts or cell phones. Things that could be stored in small spaces and moved quickly."

I exchanged glances with Herc. Oliver had definitely provided us with our next steps.

"Good job," Herc told her when she finished.

"Thanks, boss. I'm really getting the hang of the types of things you need to know in your investigations."

I was pleased with what she'd found in such a short amount of time, but since Herc had already offered his praise, I was ready to move on. "You said their finances were more difficult to check. In what way?"

"It's the girl's trust. Every penny has to be accounted for with the fiduciary but not necessarily made public. Helena Sheldon appears to have been able to snow them with the money she's taken out of the trust in the girl's name. There's no way of knowing if the girl approved these expenditures or even knows about them. Bottom line? The value of the trust was a million dollars. From what I've been able to uncover, over nine hundred and fifty thousand has been spent."

Herc blew out a breath. "Whoa! Is that even possible?"

"If the fiduciary isn't doing their job," Oliver replied. "It doesn't necessarily have to be a bank. But they have to have been appointed by the court when the will was probated. It's possible the mother was able to snow the court and get someone named who she could convince she was only acting in the girl's best interests."

"Can you find out who that is?" Herc asked.

"Oh, sure. I just hadn't gotten that far yet."

"Of course," Herc told her. "You've managed to assemble quite a bit already. How 'bout we get back together later this afternoon? You've provided us with several avenues to pursue while you continue to do your research."

She prepared to leave. "Everything's been entered into the computerized case file, in case you need to refer back to whatever."

"Boy, she's a good researcher," Herc said once it was just the two of us.

"You'll miss her once she decides she wants to go to the Academy and leave researching behind."

His eyes went wide. "Have you heard something? Last I heard, she was still debating whether or not she wanted to get her badge."

"Don't say your goodbyes yet. I haven't heard anything specific. It's just that she has to be envious about the action Dexter and Ennis, her buds, saw in our last case. And now they're off working in Vice."

He held his hands up surrender-style. "You're right. It's just that she's such a good researcher. She's relieved me of countless hours in front of the computer since she's been here."

"For now, this current case seems to be fulfilling her need to be engaged."

He set down his coffee container. "Empty. Want to go somewhere and get more while we put together our to-do list for today?"

He was putting off our analysis. Why? "Can't that wait? I'd like to get started on our list for the day now, while everything's still fresh in my brain."

"Uh, yeah. Sure. You're right. What do we do today?"

"Focus on the Sheldons, although I'm not ready to interview them again just yet. Are you?"

"No more than we need to," he replied. "What were your overall impressions?"

The amount of detail was temporarily overwhelming him.

I was about to lay out my initial impressions for him when my phone rang. "Mom? Don't panic. Ryder and I can handle this without you, but he insists you need to see it."

I hadn't even been away from the project two full days. There hadn't been time to fix all the plumbing, and the electrical hadn't even been started. What could possibly have gone wrong in that short amount of time?

"Just spit it out. Herc and I are in the middle of a conference." Not really, but I had to set boundaries. At least I kept trying.

"It's the attic again. We seem to have another unexplained happening. You have to see it for yourself. That is, if you can get away?"

"I'm not sure I can. I don't want to lose the momentum on this case. Just describe what you found."

A few beats went by. Val must be debating whether to tell me everything in lieu of my coming there to see for myself.

"Twenty-five rolls of insulation for the attic were delivered yesterday and left up there in five stacks. When we were just up there, we discovered they had been rearranged into a semi-circle of stacks of three, four, five, five, four and three with one lone roll in the center."

"A semi-circle? Is that supposed to mean something?"

"That someone could get into the house unobserved and physically move this stuff around. If it's symbolic of something more, I don't know. I just know it's got me freaked out. Ryder, too, although he's trying not to show it."

"Is that all you found?" I asked.

"Is that all?" Her voice rose volumes.

"I'm sorry, Val. I'm not trying to minimize how this must be affecting the two of you. I'm just trying to make sense of it."

"That's the thing," she replied, her tone almost normal again. "I don't think it's supposed to make sense, just shake us up. And whoever, or whatever, did this, they've succeeded."

She'd said "whatever." Granted, she'd slipped it into the rest of her comment, but did she actually think something supernatural was going on? "What do you want me to do? Besides restack them for you," I said.

"Ryder and I thought you should see this before we put them back in place."

"You couldn't just send me a photo?"

"I suppose, but you really should see this. It's just too weird."

Sometimes my role in the business was simply to provide the voice of reason when things appeared to be falling apart. This must be one of those times. "Okay. Herc and I will be there in a few minutes." I hung up and turned to Herc. "Sorry, we need to check out this incident at the Mehaffy project that has Val freaking out." I briefly described what happened.

He cocked his head, puzzled. "And they can't handle this one their own because ..."

"The house's reputation is starting to get to them. They need me to reassure them, once again, that the place isn't haunted."

"We're talking about Valerie and Ryder. Neither of them is readily susceptible to ghost stories."

"I agree. That's why we're going there to see for ourselves."

He collected our empty containers and the bag that once held our doughnuts—how did the two of us eat all those already?—and headed for the door. "I'll drive."

Ryder and Val were waiting for us in the attic when we arrived. The room didn't appear the worse for wear, except for the graduated stacks of insulation. My first impression was of some sort of monument. Herc and I just stood there taking it in, trying to make sense of it.

"We took pictures," Val said, "why, I don't know except to document this incident for future reference should we need it."

"What's your take, Ryder?" I asked. "You're not the kind of guy who lets things like this get to you."

"Something upended those rolls," he replied. "They were stacked too well. Aside from an earthquake occurring sometime last night, someone had to physically push them over. But this place was locked down tight overnight." He paused. "Something else is responsible. Something we don't know about."

"Which we've all dismissed as impossible," I said.

"Leaving the only explanation that someone got into the house," Herc said.

"But why?" Val asked.

"And how?" Ryder added.

Val continued. "That's why the two of us wanted you to see this in person. We've already tried to answer those questions without success. We hoped you might be able to answer them."

"Me? No. But it would appear that someone doesn't want us in this house. They're trying to scare us off. As for how, you two should check all the windows and doors for some means of entry that's escaped you. With anyone else, I would suggest they call in the police, and not us, to do a security check. There are people at the department who specialize in this kind of thing."

"Your mom is right," Herc said. "But if it would make you feel any more secure right now, she and I can check with your neighbors. If someone got in here last night, maybe the folks who live on either side of this house saw something suspicious."

"Why wouldn't they have let us know if they did?" Ryder asked.

Herc's suggestion we talk to the neighbors surprised me. I thought he was anxious to get back to the Craddock murder. "We won't know the answer to that until we've talked to them," I told Ryder.

Five minutes later, Herc and I stood on the front porch of the house to the right of Mehaffy House. A woman about five feet tall with a round face, round eyes and stocky body came to the door. "Yes?"

I introduced Herc and I as representatives of the police department who'd been summoned next door as a result of a break-in the night before. I chose not to mention my association with Nailed It Home Renos. "We're interviewing the neighbors to learn if you saw anything suspicious last night or any other time recently."

The woman, who introduced herself as Mrs. Alicia Hartwig, straightened her shoulders at the mention of the house next door. "No. I try to avoid anything having to do with that house. I keep the blinds drawn on all the windows on the side facing it."

That appeared to spark Herc's interest. "Oh? Why would that be, Mrs. Hartwig?" If Herc were to be thought to have a charming side, which was a stretch, he was attempting to show it now. Not that he was flirting with the woman. No, Mehaffy House seemed to be having some sort of effect on him, and he was milking this opportunity to learn as much about it as he could.

"My late husband and I moved in here after the fire next door years ago. We got this house for a song because of the stories the natives liked telling about it. We may have been able to buy this place for a lower amount, but we've paid the price otherwise over the years."

"How do you mean?" Herc asked.

She didn't invite us in, but she seemed open to further discussion. "The traffic the place next door has generated over the years has been bad enough, people showing up with their cameras and guidebooks at all times, but we've never been able to cultivate anything on that side of our house. There's plenty of sun during the day, but no plant I've ever tried to grow there has survived."

"We're sorry to hear that," Herc replied. "We understand no

one's lived in the place for years. Surely that worked to your benefit? Not having neighbors to deal with."

"You'd think so, huh? But we've put up with one nuisance after another. Loud noises in the middle of the night. Smells you wouldn't believe. And just last year they found termites on the side facing the Mehaffy place. Just that side, mind you."

Herc kept nodding like he knew exactly what she'd been going through.

When it became apparent we wouldn't be getting any hard info from her, we thanked her and headed off.

"Think we'll get the same reception at the house on the other side?" Herc asked.

"We won't know until we ask."

Just getting someone to come to the door was a challenge. We rang the doorbell twice, and when that didn't work, we knocked for several minutes. We would've given up had the blinds not been up and we thought we detected movement inside.

"Stop that noise!" A man shouted as he edged the door open a few inches. "A guy finally gets a few minutes to sleep and you have to disturb him."

He appeared to be in his late sixties, tall, unshaven, with a barrel-size chest and scruffy dark hair going gray.

"Sorry about that," I said. "We need to talk to you about the house next door or we wouldn't have disturbed you. There was some trouble over there last night. We thought perhaps you might have heard or seen something?"

"Me? No. Although with all the ruckus going on over there lately with that construction, how would I know if it was one of them or some stranger?"

"The construction crew usually clears out before six. This would've been after that. Much later, under the cover of darkness," Herc said.

The guy was shaking his head before Herc finished his sentence. "Sorry. Can't help you." The door was closed before either of us could say anything else.

"Guess that's our sign to resume our other investigation," Herc said. "At the coffee shop."

"Just one more thing. I think it's time for you to follow through on our deal. Time for your camp-out in the Mehaffy attic."

CHAPTER 13

"Hey, you two. Wait up," a woman's voice called from Mehaffy House. Harper Wickersham ran after us.

We stopped in our path and turned in unison. "Ms. Wickersham," Herc replied. "We weren't here to see you."

"I know. Valerie's been running around the house cursing all morning. I would've helped her and Ryder, but I didn't want to get any further behind on the plumbing than I already was. What's the latest on the Craddock case?"

"Translated, are you still under suspicion?" I said.

Herc didn't answer her directly. "Since you flagged us down, are you able to take a short break? We've learned some new information that's raised more questions. We were heading to the coffee shop to recharge. We could talk there," Herc told her.

"Where? I'll meet you," she replied.

Herc gave her the address.

On the way to the coffee shop, I texted Val and Ryder to update them on what, or should I say what little, we learned from the two neighbors.

Both claim they saw nothing last night. Neither particularly friendly, perhaps because they've lived here for years and aren't that crazy about anything changing next door.

Val texted back her thanks.

We were already seated with our coffee when Wickersham blew in a few minutes later. "You haven't arrested anyone else yet?" she said after she placed her order.

"Correct," Herc replied. "After we talked with you yesterday, we spent the rest of the day interviewing the occupants of the studio. Would you believe none of them stepped forward and admitted they killed your boyfriend?"

She had the grace to glance down before her next question. "When put that way, I get the picture. They're all out for themselves. But since I'm a hundred percent sure I didn't kill Jed, I'm sure it was one of them."

"Not someone else we don't know about yet?" I asked.

"I've remembered there was one other person. There was this guy he knew before he got caught up in modeling. Willis Ackroyd. He was in construction, but I doubt you'd know him. At the time, he was a finish carpenter who worked new residential construction around Orlando. He and Jed played basketball pickup games every so often. And they were both amateur magicians. They drove me crazy trying to outdo each other with their sleight-of-hand tricks when we were out together."

"Why do you think he might've killed Craddock?" Herc asked.

"There was this woman before me. Jed was up front with me about her when we first started going out. She was with Ackroyd before she met Jed and then she dumped him. Ackroyd didn't take it well."

"Love triangles happen all the time," I said. "The jilted party may be heartbroken or angry, but why do you think this guy might've wanted to kill Jed?"

"Jed was a part-time worker on my crews, but he also took part-time jobs on the crews on larger projects in Orlando. Just after he'd taken up with Ackroyd's girl, he picked up a cushy temporary project on one of those crews, a job Ackroyd apparently thought should've gone to him. He didn't like it. He threatened to make Jed's life miserable in retaliation. He didn't mention killing him, but he was serious about hurting him." She folded her hands and gazed back at us. "Does that help?"

"Possibly," I said. "Thanks. Have you remembered any more details about the folks at the studio?" I could've asked a more specific question, but at this point I wanted as much original info from her as she could come up with.

She put her elbows on the table and leaned her head into her hands.

We waited until she was ready to talk.

She didn't speak for a few beats. "I'm sorry. I want to help as much as I can, but I'm still having trouble getting past the fact he's dead. There's stuff in my head, but it's frozen for now. Give me a little more time."

"Okay," Herc told her. "Stay in touch."

"Please do the same for me once you arrest someone else."

We continued to stay at our table finishing our coffee after she took hers with her and left. "Well?" Herc asked, beating me to the punch.

"I believe her when she says she's still processing the guy's death. In the meantime, she did give us a new name. We just have to find him. Give me a minute." I grabbed my phone and pulled up a number. "Hi, this is Rowena Summerfield of Nailed It Home Renos. I'm trying to locate a finish carpenter by the name of Willis Ackroyd. Can you help me?" I listened while the woman on the other end of the line checked her database. Within a minute, I had a telephone number and an address. I turned to Herc. "I called the regional construction personnel directory and got some contact info on the guy."

"Nice going, although one of these days perhaps we should discuss the ethics of your mixing cop work with your construction ties."

He'd pushed a button I thought I'd buried. "Ethics, Herc?" My voice rose. "You're the one who keeps putting me in this position."

He bowed his head. "Yeah, I know. Cheap shot on my part."

"Yes, it was."

"Should we go find this guy or return to the analysis we started earlier?" he asked.

"Let's add one more name to our list of possible suspects." I called the number and was surprised someone answered. I'd been expecting voicemail because Ackroyd would be working.

"Hello?"

"Is this Willis Ackroyd?" I asked.

"Who wants to know?"

"I'm Rowena Summerfield. I'm a consultant to the Shasta Police Department, and my partner and I want to talk to you about the Jed Craddock murder. Where can we meet you?"

I left it up to him to cooperate. This time. Now that we knew this much about him, we could readily locate him if he failed to show up.

"We're taking a road trip," I told Herc once I hung up.

"So I gathered. Why didn't you pick somewhere closer to home?"

"Because I wasn't sure he'd come that far. I'm not sure he'll even show up now, and if he doesn't, that will suggest he knows something about this murder he doesn't want to tell us."

We reached our destination in a little over an hour, just after eleven. It was a small diner just off the Turnpike. Ackroyd hadn't shown yet. We claimed a booth midway between the entrance and the back. I ordered a plain hamburger just to be ordering. Herc's appetite had grown during the drive. He ordered a steak sandwich. The waitress had just delivered them to our booth when Ackroyd walked in.

At five-ten, unshaven with scruffy black hair, he wore a moss green knit shirt with holes and dirty blue jeans. "Okay, let's talk. This is costing me money by leaving my job behind."

"Really?" I replied. "Is that why you answered my call on the first ring? You were somewhere other than a job site waiting to get called in. What's the deal? Has work dried up for you? I understand there's plenty of new home building going on in and around Orlando these days."

He took the side of the booth opposite Herc and me, his expression challenging. "What makes you an authority on the subject? You're just cops."

"Actually, besides consulting with the police on this case, I'm actually part owner of Nailed It Home Renos and I'm quite familiar with construction in this area. Now that we've discussed my qualifications, let's talk about you and your relationship with Jed Craddock. When was the last time you saw him?"

"It's been months. We didn't part on the best of terms."

"We understand that was because the woman you'd been seeing started seeing him instead?" Herc said.

"Aren't you the diplomat?" the man said. "He stole my woman."

"And she didn't have something to do with that?" I asked.

"He snowed her with his looks."

"Who was this woman?" Herc asked.

"Why do you need her name?"

"We're just putting together a list of the people who knew him, Mr. Ackroyd. Trying to get a feel for what was happening in his life in recent months," I said.

"Krista Mowbrey," he said reluctantly. "Haven't seen her in months, either, but she used to work for Sunbright Realty."

"Thank you," I said. At that point, a thought occurred to me. Since Ackroyd wasn't working today, maybe he had money problems. That being the case, maybe he'd seen Jed Craddock more recently than he'd let on and, despite his appearance today, got the idea that his old pal might've stumbled onto a gold mine. "Perhaps you'd like to revisit your response to our question about the last time you saw Mr. Craddock? Perhaps it was a little more recent?"

Guilt flashed in his eyes. "What are you getting at?"

"I'm thinking maybe you thought if Jed Craddock could

become a male model, why couldn't you? So you went to see him to learn how to break into the business?"

He studied his hands. "I may not have that 'American Boy' look he claimed to have, but my dark looks go a long way toward making me the 'Mysterious Stranger' type."

Where had he picked up those terms? "But Craddock didn't agree, is that right?" I asked.

"He would've been admitting I could be his competition if he agreed. He was having none of my joining his agency. Wouldn't even introduce me to the owner even though he owed me."

"Owed you?" I asked.

"He stole Krista from me, then dropped her overnight when he met that plumber."

"When did you see him?" Herc asked, realizing we'd found another potential killer.

"I don't know." He shrugged. "About two weeks ago."

"You didn't get a chance to apply?" I asked.

"I should've gone to that place where he worked instead of meeting him at a nearby bar. He even suggested jobs there were scarce to discourage me."

He studied our half-eaten lunches. "Don't suppose the Shasta Police Department reimburses witnesses for lunch and gas?"

"Uh, no, not in this situation," Herc quickly replied, going into formal department mode.

"Fine, I'll catch some fast food on the way back to town." He rose and pushed away from the booth.

"We could've interviewed him over the phone," Herc said once Ackroyd left.

"No, I wanted to read his body language by seeing him in person," I answered. "I never would've thought to ask him whether he'd considered being a male model like Craddock, but I decided to ask just to hear how he'd react. He just added one more motive to the one he already had."

"I never would've made that connection, Ro. That was brilliant."

"Thanks. But unless there was more to it, Craddock's warning him off modeling doesn't seem a strong enough motive for murder."

"Not at this point," Herc said. "But if their meeting actually happened within the last two weeks, it does fall within the time period of incidents leading up to the murder."

"I think we should contact the woman, Krista Mowbrey, by phone. At some point in the last year, I suspect Craddock dumped her for Wickersham. That's a possible motive. One we shouldn't dismiss, although right now it doesn't seem to ring any bells."

CHAPTER 14

Herc picked up his partially eaten steak sandwich. "This is pretty good, but I could use something else to go along with it. Think I'll order fries."

Fries did sound good, but I went with an order of coleslaw instead.

"While we wait, we might as well get back to that briefing we were about to start when Val called us away," Herc said.

Funny how food tended to improve his analytical prowess. Was it the same when he teamed up with Al?

I returned to the section of my notebook where I'd jotted down my thoughts as Janet Oliver gave her report earlier in the day. "Two things. First, Helena Sheldon has made herself at home with Lola's trust fund, which explains how she could afford to buy that motel. That doesn't appear to fit with Craddock's murder, unless Lola has no idea what her mother's been up to and he threatened to tell her."

"It's a possibility. Meaning, we need to discover how much Lola knows and what, if anything, she's done about it."

"My vote's on her being clueless," I said.

"Mine, too, although I'm not sure we want to be the ones to

tell her, unless it's absolutely necessary to finding our killer," he replied. "What was the other thing?"

"Our first impression of Bart Sheldon was on point, only more so. He's got quite the track record with the law. Amazing that he's been able to avoid prison so long."

"He's one of those guys who can talk himself out of trouble. He looks oily; he is oily."

"Trafficking in stolen goods," I said. "Sounds like just the kind of business that might appeal to him. The robbery part in the past might've taken too much brain power and energy, so instead, he turned to receiving what others took, storing it until the heat died down and then turning it over to whoever was moving it. If our read on him is correct, he probably only exerted himself enough to open a door in some storeroom, let someone else move it in and move it out and collect his due for the low risk he took keeping it out of sight."

"Good summary, but if he's been continuing to receive stolen property, why does the studio appear to be in financial trouble?" he asked.

One answer seemed obvious. "My guess is that he hasn't put any of this money into keeping the place going. Helena Sheldon may not even know what he's been up to."

"If you're right, that puts a strange twist on this case. She might be inadvertently shielding him," he said.

"We need to wait for Oliver to learn more about the trust fund fiduciary, but we could do some reconnaissance at the motel and see if we could locate potential hiding places."

His forehead wrinkled in thought. "We'll probably need a warrant for that, which means we'd need to spell out what we're seeking."

"We're not ready to do that," I replied. "I don't want to tip him off too soon."

"He's probably gotten rid of any damning evidence," he pointed out. "All we could do is case the place for potential hiding places."

"We need a blueprint," I said. "Let's call our friends at the city building inspection office and see what they can do for us." A while back, we'd investigated the case of a murdered city building inspector. Although we interviewed the entire staff, the killer turned out to be someone else. Hopefully, we hadn't burned too many bridges there.

I put in a call to Vincent Donahue at the city's building inspection office. He'd been the most forthcoming with our questions. "Hi, Vince. This is Rowena Summerfield." I reminded him of the case concerning Mortimer Fonseca, the fellow building inspector who'd been murdered months before. Then I asked for his help finding a blueprint of the Sheldon Studio. "If there's nothing on file, perhaps there's something for the Starlight Motel, what the complex was previously."

He agreed to see what he could find but warned it might take several hours, especially if whatever they had in their files hadn't been digitalized.

I thanked him and hung up. I returned my attention to Herc. "Let's put the two Sheldons aside for now and continue digging deeper for our other suspects, primarily Compton and Drysdale," I said.

"Should we have Oliver switch over to them?"

"We could tackle them ourselves while she concentrates on the two areas she's already checking. They both must have websites showing off their work."

"I guess it's as good as anything before we interview them again. We need to go armed with more info about their backgrounds this time around," he said.

While we drove back to Shasta, I checked out the two websites.

Joel Drysdale's modeling history went further back than Compton's. He first worked out of a small agency in Miami doing primarily local TV commercials and runway shows. He was with them four years, then he became a free agent for a couple of years. He was the first one hired by the Sheldons two years ago. He described himself as senior model and training manager for the Sheldon Studio.

The website did exactly what it was supposed to do: promote him through his portfolio and provide contact information to others who might be interested in hiring him. In other words, it didn't shed much light on the man himself, although it did give us one more piece of information we didn't have before, the name of his former employer. I made a note and then proceeded to Compton's page.

The layout of Compton's page looked similar to Drysdale's. The Sheldons must've taken care of both. The appearance and appeal were the most important features. Although I was no expert in the area, since Nailed It Home Renos had its own website, I'd had to learn the ins and outs of their composition. These were pretty ordinary. Perhaps one of the reasons why the Sheldons weren't getting as much business as they hoped.

"Whatcha finding?" Herc asked. "Anything that says, 'Watch this guy. He has murderous tendencies'?"

"Not exactly. In my opinion, both websites are pretty milquetoast. I did find the name of Drysdale's former employer. I'm going to call them now."

"Margaret Kane Modeling Agency," the woman on the other end of the line said.

I explained who I was and asked to speak with the person in charge.

"That would be me, Jessica Kane."

"Who's Margaret Kane?" I asked.

"She's the founder, now retired," Jessica Kane told me. "You're with the police in Shasta?"

"That's correct. My partner and I are investigating the murder of a local man, a male model with the Sheldon Studio. I understand another member of that group, Joel Drysdale, used to model for your group. Is that correct?"

"For legal purposes, I can only give you so much information about prior employees, especially over the phone, but yes, he was an employee."

"I understand, although we can subpoena additional information if necessary. Can you tell me what kind of model he was?"

"He didn't work steadily, but he showed up for whatever jobs he was assigned, and his clients seemed reasonably satisfied with his work." She provided the months and years of his employment, three years and ten months.

"What were the circumstances of his leaving?" I asked.

"He left on his own accord, saying he'd received enough training from us that he felt comfortable going out on his own. That's about all I can tell you."

"He later was hired by the Sheldon Studio as not only their senior model but also their training manager. In your opinion, was he qualified for the latter?" I was pushing, but I wanted to find out how much she'd say.

"I can't really speak to that. He never functioned as a trainer for us. You'd have to learn from the Sheldon people how well he's been doing in that capacity."

I had to hand it to her. She was very good at administrative-speak. About the only additional information she'd given me was to verify his period of employment. At least what he had on his website was legit.

Still, I had to try for more. "You've been very helpful, Ms. Kane." Flatter, appear satisfied, then pounce. "Is there anything else you can tell me about Joel Drysdale?"

She didn't reply at first. I was ready to concede until she spoke again. "My mother's trusted right hand, Eloise George, retired a few years back. She might be able to give you more specific information about him. I no longer have contact information for her, but she lives up the coast in Palm Bay."

Eureka! You never know when you'll strike gold. I thanked her and ended the call.

I dipped into the statewide vehicle registration database, hoping it would be that easy to find Eloise George. I found an E.

George and called that number. It turned out to be for an Edward George, but Eloise was his mother. "She remarried two years ago and now goes by Eloise Lopez," he told me.

Eloise Lopez answered on the second ring. Once again, I went through my introduction and the reason for my call, telling her I was putting her on speaker so my partner, Hercules Morgan, could hear as well.

"How is Joel doing these days? I've often wondered if he was able to come back after his bad luck."

Though I wanted to pounce on that statement, I first updated her about his current situation, neglecting to tell her he was a suspect in a murder case. "What do you mean by 'his bad luck'?" I asked, having dispensed with the niceties first.

"Perhaps I misspoke when I characterized it as 'bad luck.' 'Poor judgment' might be more on point. He was caught taking home with him one of the outfits he wore in a shoot for a major clothing retailer. He claimed he'd been told by the other two men on the shoot that the retailer was giving one outfit to each of the models in hopes they'd wear it to promote the retailer's product. Of course, that wasn't the case. He was picked up on two security cameras with the goods and immediately charged with theft."

"You used the word 'claimed.' I'm guessing he was set up by the other two models or someone else on the shoot," I said.

"You're way ahead of me. Although we tried to encourage a spirit of camaraderie amongst our people, a competitive atmosphere permeated the place. There was a lot of jockeying for assignments that would produce the most attention. Joel's star was on the rise at the time, which made him a target of his peers. He couldn't prove his innocence, but Margaret was anxious to avoid a scandal that would reflect poorly on the agency, so our folks worked a deal with the police and the retailer to get the charges dropped if Joel paid for the clothing.

"But the stench of wrongdoing wouldn't go away. He got progressively fewer jobs. That part concerned Margaret, because it affected our bottom line. But she wasn't convinced he'd purposely stolen the goods. He'd been the dupe of the other two models, who'd played on his poor judgment and greed. She called him in for a heart-to-heart and suggested it was time for him to reshape his image by becoming a free agent. He left within the month. I suspect she offered to throw some business his direction for a limited period if he went." She stopped, apparently having shared as much as she wanted to say. "That's all I can tell you about Joel. Like I said, I hope he's doing well these days."

"Thank you. We appreciate your willingness to talk to us," I said. Her recollection of Drysdale's departure from his former employer hinted at why he now found himself working for a less successful operation than he'd enjoyed in Miami.

"Did that tell you what you wanted to know?" she asked.

Herc took this one. "Yes, thank you. You added to our information." Although my number would've appeared on her screen, he repeated it should something else occur to her.

"Her story portrays Joel Drysdale in a slightly different light than he told us," I said once the call had ended. "I suspected his career had taken a wrong turn sometime in the past to have brought him from the major market of Miami to the smaller market of Shasta. Now we know."

"If we can trust what Eloise Lopez told us," Herc said. "Maybe he really did steal those clothes and bluffed it out as long as he could. The employer may not have gotten him off just to save her agency the scandal, like Lopez says, but simply waited until the fireworks died down to get rid of him."

"I suppose that line of thinking is possible too." I chuckled. "Nice to see Hercules Morgan the Cynic is back."

He started. "Whattaya mean? I didn't think he'd left."

"Maybe not, but lately it seems you've mellowed a bit. I thought perhaps that was due to Luann Cory."

He shot a me quick look. "Luann? All I did was invite her to Thanksgiving dinner at Val's. Took pity on her being alone otherwise."

"Oh. My mistake," I said with mock sincerity.

"When would I have seen her? You and I've been tied up with this case almost every day since then."

"Not last weekend? It would've been so easy to suggest a movie or dinner," I replied.

"Get real, Ro. There were back-to-back football games all weekend. Both college and pro. When I took her home I found out she's not a fan of the sport, thinking she might want to watch a couple with me. And she'd already made plans with some friend to attend a holiday bazaar." He shook his shoulders. "Yuck."

"Your invitation was sorta last minute, Herc. Maybe next time you could ask at least a week in advance."

"Next time? Stop playing matchmaker. I tried and struck out. End of story."

I studied him through hooded eyes. Was he serious or just licking his wounds? What wounds? He'd asked at the last minute, probably so he wouldn't appear too anxious. She didn't like football, and she'd made other plans.

Then I got this brilliant idea. Beware of brilliant ideas. I knew that. Too many of my past trial balloons had burst right after liftoff. Some before they ever got launched. Nevertheless, nothing ventured …

"Now that I'm helping you on this case, and given whatever happened to the rolls of insulation in the attic of Mehaffy House, it's time for you to make good on our agreement, your sleepover."

"You're really going to hold me to that?"

"What do you think?"

"This case is taking a lot out of me. Since it's Friday, I was hoping you'd let me off the hook so I could set myself in front of my TV tonight with a couple brewskies."

"It's just midafternoon. What say we pack it in early so you can have some down time before you and your bedroll settle in for the night?"

He scowled. "You're a real buzzkill."

Now that we'd gotten this far, time to launch Part B of my

idea. "Perhaps the prospect of ghostbusting would be more appealing if you had company?"

He brightened. "You gonna join me?"

"Me? No. I was thinking of Luann."

"You just got done scolding me for asking her to watch the football games so late last weekend. Asking for tonight is even worse."

"But you have an excuse, this morning's incident with the insulation. The sooner we can get to the bottom of this haunted house thing, the better."

He frowned. "You don't seriously think someone or something is haunting that house, do you?

"No, I don't think it's some ethereal being that did it. But someone knocked those rolls of insulation over. I'd sure like to know how it happened."

"But if I'm there protecting the house, won't that scare away whoever it was? Or is that your intent?" he asked.

"I want to debunk this haunted house rumor once and for all to keep my crews on the job if anyone is worried about ghosts."

"Say I did invite Luann. Wouldn't I be putting her in danger if someone does show up?"

Interesting point. Maybe I shouldn't be playing Cupid when there was a remote possibility of danger. Like I said, beware of brilliant ideas. "I suppose that's a possibility, although don't firefighters go through some kind of self-defense training? And firefighters face more danger than we do." I shrugged. "It was just a suggestion. Use your own judgment. But I still hope you will stake out the place."

He didn't say no, but he didn't say yes. I'd have to wait and see.

CHAPTER 15

got back to my duplex around three thinking Jason would be delighted. I didn't usually roll in until between five and six.

I set about finding his special bag of treats, the one I kept high up in the cupboard following an incident some time ago when my resourceful cat managed to knock the bag off the countertop and broke it open. When offered the opportunity, Jason knows no bounds. His gluttony resulted in an expensive trip to the vet.

A rationed number of treats sat out waiting for him for over ten minutes before I started to worry about a repeat of yesterday's disappearance. What was going on?

I tried calling to him several times. Val and I hadn't found his hiding place when we'd searched the place thoroughly the night before, but I needed to do something to keep myself busy, so I checked the closets, looked under the beds, rummaged through the dirty laundry and made sure he wasn't in the bathtub or shower. I had no idea how he would've gotten into the shower, but he was an ingenious cat, and if his main goal right now was to stay hidden, he might've figured out some way to open the door.

As I hunted him, I searched for traces of cat vomit or hairballs. I didn't know whether to be excited or not when I didn't find any.

I returned to the kitchen. Maybe he'd come running if he heard the sound of me working with his dishes.

I debated calling Val, but her day had been interrupted enough. Instead, I called the vet. I'd held back calling Dr. Gardiner the day before, but two days in a row of Jason making himself scarce told me something definitely was amiss.

"Describe what's been happening," Dr. Gardiner said after I briefly summarized the reason for my call.

"There's not that much to tell, which makes this all the more concerning to me," I said and gave her a blow-by-blow recap.

"How long did you say it took him to show up last night?"

"Close to half an hour. In Jason Time, when it's time to eat, that's eons."

"And this hasn't happened before?"

"No."

"I'm reading through his file as we speak. You estimate he's about four and a half years old?"

"Based on your examination of him when my friend Ryder Tompkins first found him. He was a mature young male at that time, in basically good shape, although he'd been fending for himself for some time. Still, he wasn't feral. He'd come from a home somewhere. No one ever claimed him even though we advertised for several weeks."

"He must have some pretty secure hiding spots if you haven't been able to find him. For now, I'd advise a glass of wine, if you've got some on hand."

"Wine?"

"Unorthodox, I know," she said. "But it doesn't sound like you'll find him on your own until he's ready to be found. The wine will help you relax while you wait."

"What do you think is wrong with him?" I asked.

"No idea, Rowena. Bring him in tomorrow once he has shown up."

I got off the phone feeling worse than before I called. On second thought, why not take her up on her informal prescription? Five minutes later, I collapsed on the love seat in my living room, a glass of chardonnay in my hand. Five minutes after that, I was no longer blaming Dr. Gardiner for not treating her patient. She'd effectively treated the patient's keeper. At least temporarily.

Wine consumed, I checked to see if Vince Donahue had sent the blueprints for the motel yet. I was on my way to my notebook computer when who should appear but the reason for my drinking.

Was I supposed to make a fuss over him and tell him how much I was happy to see him, or should I scold him for frightening me so? I went with Good Mother for now. Until Dr. Gardiner had checked him out, I needed to keep things positive.

I waited until after he'd feasted to look him over. I didn't find anything.

What was going on with my pet? For being so smart otherwise, why couldn't he exercise a little of that intelligence now and clue me in on his issues?

Before I reviewed the blueprints, which had now arrived in my file, I did an internet search for reasons why cats might hide, even missing regular meal times. I skipped over the physical ailments, thinking I'd leave that to the vet the next day. I was more intrigued by the types of psychological problems cats might experience. I had no idea there was such a body of information about the subject, although given how human Jason acted at times, I shouldn't have been surprised.

I read that cats can suffer both depression and anxiety for a variety of reasons, particularly changes in their environment like a move, a new baby or new pet, or traumatic events like a death in the family. None of those fit Jason's case. But that didn't mean something wasn't affecting him negatively. I just had to get a little more creative in my thinking.

My better judgment told me it wasn't because Chuck had moved in, although that event fit the list of possibilities. Chuck had been a regular overnight visitor for some time. And he'd moved in a month ago. If that had bothered Jason, why had this behavior shown up only in the last two days? Actually, once we'd decided to live together, Chuck had wanted Jason and me to relocate to his larger home or for us to find a new place. I'd argued for staying here to spare Jason from having to adjust to a new home.

I tried to think back over recent interactions between Jason and Chuck. I couldn't come up with any negative issues. Jason didn't run away from Chuck or hiss at him or attempt to scratch him. He didn't exactly cuddle up to Chuck, but he did let Chuck pet him.

But if not Chuck, what? Last month, Chuck and I had been on the road searching for Ryder's sister for a number of days, but Jason took his mad out on us when we first returned home. Since then, he'd been fine.

Coming up blank, I decided to switch gears and check out the motel blueprints Donahue had sent. Once I got my bearings, what I saw was pretty much what I remembered from yesterday. Five rooms were located on both the second and first floors of the residential end. We'd visited three on the second floor, Craddock's, Compton's and Drysdale's. That left two on that floor we hadn't seen and five on the first floor yet to be checked. The original plans indicated more rooms in the main area of the building than we'd viewed. Apparently some walls had been removed to create the meeting room and training area. The same for the fitness room, the main apartment and Lola's mini-suite.

If I wanted to hide goods of indeterminate size, where would I put them? Due to the number of entrances around the building, there were too many choices without more personal observation. And as we'd already discussed, that would require a warrant. We weren't ready to tip our hand until we knew more.

I was just winding up my review of the blueprints when Chuck walked in. He offered a tentative smile. "You're home early. Find your killer already?"

"Don't I wish. We broke early so Herc could rest up before his stakeout at Mehaffy House tonight. I returned home too. I had some work I could do here, but it got put on hold until Jason showed up. He pulled the same stunt today."

"Stunt? You mean he disappeared again?"

I nodded. "I searched the house again and like last night couldn't find him. This time I called Dr. Gardiner. She advised me to pour myself a glass of wine and relax until Jason appeared, since I couldn't do anything else. Then she made an appointment for me to bring our boy in tomorrow to determine if there's any physical reason for this behavior."

"Good. The doctor knows best."

"Just in case it isn't anything physical, since I can't seem to find anything wrong with him, I've been reading up on psychological traumas in cats." I wasn't sure if he'd laugh or pooh-pooh me, but I thought he should know.

"That's an interesting possibility. Did you discuss that idea with Dr. Gardiner?"

"No, I wanted to get her assessment of Jason's physical condition first."

"Good plan."

I went over what I'd read in one of the articles. "Change seems to be a major factor in depression or anxiety in cats. The only change around here, Chuck, has been you moving in."

"But that was several weeks ago, and his disappearing act didn't start until yesterday."

"That's what I've been telling myself," I said. "That as well as remembering how well the two of you have been getting on."

"But he did come out of hiding finally, right?"

"Yes, as if nothing had happened. It's so weird."

"We can't do anything more tonight unless his behavior changes. We'll just have to watch him," he said. "As much as he'll allow."

While we prepared our evening meal, I asked about his day.

"Shane Bolton, my manager at The Sandpiper, asked me to stop by this afternoon. He needed to vent. He's down two wait staff and is worried he is about to lose another one. Wanted to ask if I thought his management style was working against him."

"Shane questioning his management style? I find that difficult to believe. What did you tell him?"

"Started by telling him I was surprised to learn he's losing people as well as hearing him questioning his management skills. I wanted him to know I had no reason to doubt his abilities as a manager. That said, I asked him why he thought he might be the problem. Had those who'd quit said as much?"

"Good. You put it back on him."

"He said the reason wasn't money for either. One got a similar job on the other side of town, closer to where she lives. The other is leaving town because her husband got a promotion to a position in Tampa."

"He couldn't have done anything about either of them," I said.

"Which is what I told him. But Shane was on the blame train, focusing primarily on himself, which is when it occurred to me this wasn't about the people who'd quit on him. Something was up with him himself. But I knew if I said, 'What's up with you, dude?' he'd deny anything was bothering him."

"What did you do?"

"I hadn't realized until then just how much I'd learned listening to you question the folks we interviewed while we searched for Melinda. I started on the perimeter with a couple broad-based questions and gradually worked toward the center. Turns out he's been talking to Lorna Varney and is interested in being considered for her job when she leaves."

"That's news. I was aware she only signed on for a short but undetermined stint to manage the wine bar after consulting on its development, but I didn't know she'd decided on an end date."

"She hasn't, as far as I know. It's just her way of reminding me how valuable she is. Apparently she and Shane have been talking from time to time, and he's come away with the impression she'll be leaving soon. When that happens, he thinks he'd like to take over for her."

"How do you feel about that?" I asked him.

"You don't want to comment, I take it?"

"My opinion isn't what counts here, Chuck."

He sank onto a kitchen chair. "He caught me off guard. I haven't pictured him in that role, but if I'm honest with myself, I think that's because I'm so pleased with what he's been doing managing the restaurant, I didn't want to consider him doing something else. The renovated Sandpiper hasn't been operational that long. I guess I wanted him to stick around a couple of years at least."

"That's a fair assumption," I replied. "How do the two jobs compare? Is one more difficult than the other, more valuable?"

He took some time to consider my questions. "Apples and oranges, Ro. They may seem similar, but they call for different types of skills. The restaurant client base is more varied, requiring a manager who can relate to all types. Plus, the menu is broader. The staff and client base are larger. The wine bar's clientele is narrower but more demanding. The restaurant manager can fall back on the chef's staff for food expertise. The wine bar manager is the knowledge lynchpin there. Currently, they're both receiving about the same salaries and perks."

"If Shane is seeking more money or more responsibility, it would appear he wouldn't get that by taking over Lorna's position. But if he wants to broaden his knowledge and skill base, the move might be good for him."

"Wow," he said after I finished. "Every crook and killer within a thousand miles should be quaking in their boots. You are so good at reading people and situations."

I had to chuckle. "Just a thousand miles? Why not the whole country?"

Now he chuckled.

"But seriously, I'm glad if I helped you see things more clearly, since I can't seem to figure out my own cat's problem."

"Rowena, I am so sorry. Here I've been going on about my personnel problems when I should've been more sensitive to the story of our feline landlord." He rose and pulled me into his arms and kissed my hair. The scent of his cedarwood aftershave was comforting. So much better than Joel Drysdale's overpowering lemongrass. "I won't try to tell you to stop worrying, but I can do my best to help you relax. Let's go to our room. The meal can wait. And Jason's fine for the night."

CHAPTER 16

Chuck's ministrations helped my mood considerably. By the time I dropped off to sleep, though still worried about my furry housemate, I felt more prepared to deal with whatever Dr. Gardiner found. I texted Val to update her and ask if she could go with me to the vet the next morning. I hadn't wanted to worry her until then.

The next morning, the first order of business was to get Jason ready for transport. Since I rarely traveled with him, Jason knew the carrier meant the vet's office and a lot of prodding, poking and maybe even a shot, the one thing he hated more than my multiday absences. As soon as he figured out what was on the docket, he'd turn into a different animal.

Through hit and miss, Val and I had developed a certain procedure over the years for getting him ready for the trip. The night before an appointment, I removed his food bowl, although I left his water bowl out. Early that morning, while I held him, cooing sweet nothings, Val put his open carrier on the kitchen floor and placed a full bowl of food inside.

I didn't trust Jason to enter the carrier voluntarily. He'd disappear to places unknown as soon as I put him down. But getting him into the carrier was not fun. Though ninety percent of his time was spent lazing around and napping, my cat possessed a spectacular set of muscles that all engaged at times like this. To say it was a struggle was an understatement.

But we finally succeeded. The return trip from the vet's office would be easier, because he knew from past experience home was on the other end of his two-way ticket.

Dr. Gardiner had a way with animals. Though not quite Dr. Doolittle, she could still talk to them and get them to relax enough so she could examine them. Jason was no exception. I released the breath I must've been holding until he settled down. No purrs yet, but the wild animal I'd fought with just a half hour before had disappeared.

"Everything seems to be in order," she told us once finished checking him out. "He might be putting on a little extra weight but only a few ounces right now. Just watch him. You've probably been urging him to come out of hiding with those special treats I advised be doled out sparingly."

Boy, did she have me pegged. "Physically, he's okay then?" I asked.

"Right. But I'm glad you brought him in just to eliminate that as a possibility."

"Which lands us right back at a psychological reason," Val said.

"That would appear to be the case," Dr. Gardiner said. "Describe once again the behavior you've observed in him."

"He just fails to appear for a much longer period than what's his custom," I replied. "So far, only when I first get home. The first day, that was around five. Yesterday, it was just after three."

"And this has never been his pattern before?" she asked.

"No," I returned.

"Anything new going on in your household?" she asked next. I related what I'd told Chuck the night before. "So nothing major in the last several days?" she said when I finished.

"Not unless cause and effect takes a few weeks to build in cats," I replied.

She tilted her head, considering. "Not that I've ever run across, but I'm not dismissing the possibility. What did you say he did once he showed himself? Anything different there?"

"Nothing noticeable."

"Hmm. Right now, there isn't much I can tell you, since this has only been going on two days. I'll write you a scrip for mild tranquilizers should you feel they are necessary in the days ahead. Right now, it doesn't sound like he needs medication. Use them sparingly, if you do decide to try them."

I couldn't help wondering if the meds were more for my benefit than Jason's.

We thanked her and packed Jason up to leave.

"Will you still be working on your case today?" Val asked on the way home.

"I want to hear how Herc's night in the attic went, but unless something new comes up in the next two days, we're putting off further interviews until Monday. You're welcome to sit in when I get my report, unless he's already contacted you?" I asked.

"Haven't heard from him, and yes, I'd like to be there. Is he coming to your place?"

"Actually, I've made plans to meet him for coffee once I got Jason home. Chuck had to check on some things at the deli this morning, but he'll be back the rest of the day. Someone will be there for Jason most of the day. I have no idea if our presence will make things better or worse."

Herc was waiting for us at the coffee shop when we arrived an hour later. "Mornin', ladies. Isn't it a beautiful day?"

Val and I exchanged looks. "I guess. Sounds like it's much more beautiful for you. Should we attribute your mood to your stay at Mehaffy House last night? You did stay all night, I hope?" I said.

He nodded, a huge non-Herc-like smile taking over his face. "Of course! That was the deal, as I recall. I'm pleased to report we saw no ghosts or any other beings. No windows opening on their own accord or rolls of insulation toppling over and getting rearranged. However, sometime around one thirty we did think we heard a sound on the one side of the house near the door. But by the time we got down there, we saw nothing."

"A lot of 'we's' in that statement, my friend," I said. "Would I be correct in assuming you were not alone?"

He offered us a sly smile, like we'd picked up on some huge secret. "As a matter of fact, I followed your suggestion and invited Luann to join me. I told her you thought I should have someone else with me for verification purposes should something weird turn up. She loved the idea, even brought a picnic basket complete with checked tablecloth."

I held up my coffee cup to him. "We are so proud of you."

"And happy for you," Val added. "It's about time."

His expression morphed to one of his patented insulted grimaces. "Valerie! I never gave you a hard time when you started seeing Watkins."

"You just don't remember," she replied, smiling. "So? Tell us about your evening with Luann Cory."

"She brought her own bedroll. I bought two cots to place them on and set them several feet apart, if you must know."

"We mustn't," I said. "TMI. Tell us about your surveillance activity."

He put down his coffee cup and took a bite of one the two blueberry muffins he'd ordered. "Uh, right. For starters, the neighbor on the north side of the house knew we were there from the minute we arrived. With all the gear and food we had with us, I had to park in front of the house. He was outside when we got there and came right over while we unloaded. Asked if we were a late crew for those two madwomen tearing the house apart. He was concerned we'd make noise while he was watching his game. Most of the evening was uneventful from the standpoint of unexplained phenomena or noises."

"What about from the standpoint of you and Luann getting to know each other better?" Val asked.

I was glad she'd come along. We could double-team me with questions about his "date."

"That part was … okay," he replied. "More than, if you must know, but that's my business."

"Your business?" I said. "Since when have you been so protective of your love life?"

He studied his hands. "Don't call it that. At least not yet. All you two need to know is that when we weren't checking out the house, we had some nice conversations. Got to know each other a lot better."

"I'm glad that part worked well for you, Herc," I said. "Thank you for taking up the challenge. It sounds like the house may only be haunted in urban myth."

"Not quite so fast, Ro. I told you about what sounded like a noise outside in the early morning hours. Luann and I went downstairs to check it out but couldn't find anything. I even went outside, but I had to wait until this morning to look for footprints and any other indication someone had been there. Nothing."

"Are you sure you heard something?" Val asked.

"We both thought so, but neither of us could swear to it a hundred percent."

"Maybe whoever has been trying to gaslight us knew you were there and put their act on hold until you left," I said, trying to grasp what had been happening. "You said the neighbor on the north side knew you were there. He may not have thought you were there for the night to ghost-bust, but all he had to do was see your car still out on the street."

"Then why the noise?" he asked. "I said I can't swear to it, but I'm pretty sure I heard something."

"Could be someone was playing with you," Val said. "Offered

just enough evidence of some kind of presence to keep you, us, wondering."

"Not sure I see it like that," he said. "Pretty far-fetched, and your mom knows I'm not much of a woo-woo guy. I need hard facts to convince me of anything, and since I don't have any of that to offer up from last night's surveillance, what do you guys plan to do next?"

I eyed my daughter. She spoke first. "I say we proceed full speed ahead and forget the idea the house is haunted."

"And if there's another incident like the rolls of insulation?" I asked.

"Then we deal with whatever it is when that happens," she said.

"I agree with Val," Herc said as he finished his first muffin. "Luann and I used our stay last night as a chance to inspect what you've got going in that place. Even though the interior has been stripped bare, she was quite impressed. And she knows her structures. She can't wait to see it once you're done."

"We'll definitely give her an advance showing," I said.

He stuck the remaining muffin into a paper bag. "My report delivered, think I'll be taking off. I didn't get much sleep last night, and not for the reason you think. Luann and I had a very nice evening. I'm glad I asked her to join me."

No need to remind him it had been my suggestion. He just wanted to come off looking like he was in charge.

"I forwarded that blueprint we received from Vince Donahue to you last night," I said. "You probably didn't have a chance to look into it, but maybe you can review it sometime this weekend. Let's meet up at the station first thing Monday morning and lay out our plan for second interviews."

"Sounds like a plan," he said.

"He couldn't get out of here fast enough," Val said once Herc had left.

I'd noticed that too. "You don't suppose he's meeting up with Luann later today?"

"I may have suggested he invite her to Thanksgiving dinner, but you're the one who put them together house-sitting last night. Be ready, Mom. You may have set something in motion you'll never again be able to control."

That thought had already occurred to me. Val saying it out loud made it real. What had I done?

CHAPTER 17

Even though Chuck and I stayed home the rest of the weekend, Jason still pulled his disappearing act both on Saturday and Sunday. By then, we were becoming more accustomed to this behavior but by no means accepting it. Once he reappeared again each time, he showed no signs of discomfort or fear.

"If you really want to know where he's hiding out," Chuck said, "we could get one of those small video cameras and attach it to his collar."

I seriously considered the idea, but I asked myself if that was more to address my own curiosity about where he was hiding than to figure out what was causing him to hide so frequently. "Let's give it a few more days. If this new behavior continues, then I want to know what's causing it."

By Monday morning, I was coping better with Jason's vanishing act and ready to dig in to find Craddock's killer. I was on my way to the station, having purchased a half dozen bagels, when Herc called. "Slight change in plans. Thought our brains might perk up if we changed our environment. Meet me at Pillsbury Park. It's just down the street from the Sheldon Studio."

"Okay but why? Who are you hiding out from at the station?"

"Why are you always so suspicious, Rowena?"

"Al is coming in today, isn't he? Is he done with his assignment in Orlando?"

Brief silence while Herc probably decided whether to come clean about Al. "Just for today. The team in Orlando got called away on another assignment. They're supposed to be back tomorrow."

"Okay. I'll see you there in ten. I've got a half dozen bagels and coffee for myself."

"I'll take care of mine, and Oliver will bring her own."

I beat Herc to the park. I was already seated at a picnic table bench when he arrived.

Janet Oliver was coming. She must have new info for us. Which she got right to once she and Herc joined me at the picnic table I'd claimed. For late November, the weather was still warm and humid. Maybe, despite Al's presence, we should meet back at the station or go to my duplex. As the sun rose, it would only get warmer. Uncomfortably warm. My mental acuities dip when I perspire.

A couple of honey bees circled the box of bagels. Hungry or just curious? None of the contents were sweet. And as always, my coffee was black. Perhaps Herc's strong cologne would scare them away. When did he start wearing cologne? Well, duh.

"Hope you left a few of those babies in the box for us," Herc said.

"You'll have to fight the bees for them, but yes, I've only had one on the way here."

That was all the invitation he needed to swoop in, grab a couple and hand one to Oliver.

"Thanks, Mrs. Summerfield," Janet Oliver said, accepting the offered bagel and slipping nimbly over the bench. Herc made quick work of his bagel before attempting to sit. After one botched try to mount the bench himself, he moved to the end and settled there.

Herc devoured another goodie before shifting into investigation mode. "Okay, before those bees swoop in, let's get into this. Oliver wanted to wait until you joined us before updating me on the additional info she's come upon. So, Janet, the floor is yours."

She wiped a few bagel crumbs from her face with a tissue she'd retrieved from her purse before turning on her notebook computer. "I'll start with the financial information first. The fiduciary for Lola Benson's trust fund is a Janelle Norris, Helena Sheldon's mother and Lola's grandmother."

"Grandmother? Is that even legal?" I asked.

"That was my first reaction too," she replied. "I called a banker friend to check. Apparently almost anyone can be fiduciary as long as named by the deceased in the insurance documents and approved by the court following a review of their background. I couldn't find too much on her personal life other than she lives on the edge of the law but has never been sentenced. Helena Sheldon is her only child and Lola her only grandchild. She receives a small stipend for serving as fiduciary, which is about all the income she has, although I found a few cash deposits during the last few years."

"Any idea where they came from?" Herc asked.

"No."

Herc turned to me. "We were planning to interview Helena Sheldon again, but this adds another detail to the mix."

"Already noted," I replied.

"I was also able to unearth more information about the Sheldons' finances, both personal and related to the studio. At the time of the murder, their joint savings account showed two hundred fifteen dollars. Both have separate accounts as well. Hers held two thousand four hundred seventy-five dollars and twenty cents. His held eighteen dollars and forty-one cents. As of the close of business this past Thursday, which was the most recent data I could get and two days after the murder, the joint account now holds one hundred ninety-seven dollars. Hers and his have remained the same."

"In other words," I said, "their accounts weren't immediately affected by the murder."

"They appear to have been living off their credit cards, at least for day-to-day essentials like food and gas," she said. "Nothing major or unusual. Pretty much that way for the last six months as well as the two years and one month they've been in operation. The real expenditures have been addressed with their joint checking account for the studio. I put together spreadsheets for all of this data, which is already in the case file."

"Thanks, Oliver," Herc said. "Your help in these areas is invaluable. It used to take me forever to track down this kind of thing before you came along."

"You're welcome, Lieutenant. Don't put yourself down. I know what a stickler for specifics you are, and you didn't have a lot of the technical tools then like I have at my disposal now."

I remembered the days when Herc would spend hours poring over paper reports and agonizing until he balanced everything, which didn't always happen because someone was cheating the system and hiding money. Those exercises in futility put him in less than positive moods, which weren't fun for any of us. I silently thanked the arrival in our lives of Janet Oliver and modern technology. The combo gave Herc and me more time to focus on the less financial aspects of cases.

"I have more to report," she went on. "Lola Benson was asked to leave school; that's being kind. She was expelled for selling stolen goods. Since she was underage, she was given probation and sent home and placed under her parents' watchful eyes. That last part was me being cynical, given what we're learning about Helena and Bart Sheldon."

"So it wasn't boyfriend problems that sent her over the brink," Herc said.

"Or the boyfriend got her to do it," I said. "What kind of stolen goods? Did you get those details?"

"Cell phones."

Herc repeated her words. "As in the same kind of stolen goods Bart Sheldon has been associated with?"

"I couldn't find a direct link, probably because Bart Sheldon's role in moving stolen goods has never been proven and Lola Benson refused to reveal where she got the cell phones."

"It appears there's more to Lola Benson than we initially thought, although we didn't hear about the rivalries amongst the men until we talked to her," I said.

Oliver switched to another page on her notebook. "You'll also want to talk to the two male models again. Both brought their own baggage to Sheldon Studio."

"Do tell," I said, although I'd already done my own research on the two men.

"Trey Compton got into trouble in high school because he fought some school bullies. Some wise judge sentenced him to community service doing janitorial work at a local gym, where he got interested in body building. He was on his way to state champion when the Sheldons found him and convinced him to join their new enterprise instead. He gave up prize money worth several thousand dollars as well as potential contracts with various businesses in exchange for a modeling career that apparently hasn't produced the fame and wealth he anticipated."

"Interesting, but why would that be a motive for killing Craddock?" Herc asked.

"Oliver's just reporting the facts, Herc. It's up to us to either connect them to the murder or not," I told him.

"Yeah, sure. Sorry, Janet. Didn't mean to put down all your hard work."

"It's okay, Lieutenant. I know how you, uh, work."

"How about Drysdale?" I asked. "I already talked to someone who knew him at the agency in Miami, but the more information about then or more recent, the better."

"I have more recent info. His checking account dipped to almost zero in the last six months. He didn't have much there in the first place. No more than seven hundred dollars. Numerous withdrawals of fifty and seventy-five dollars at a time. I wasn't able to uncover what they were for, but if the guy was down to his last bucks, that could be a motive for murder."

"Funny how none of this came out when we interviewed those two guys," I said.

"You know as well as I, we rarely get all the information from first interviews," Herc said.

Oliver shifted position. "That's it for my report. Oh, wait, I have contact info for Krista Mowbrey. Last known address, which I can't swear by, and a telephone number." She texted those to us. "Anything else I should be researching?"

Herc raised a brow my direction. "I can't think of anything at the moment," I replied.

"We'll text if anything else comes up from our second inter-views," Herc told her.

She stood and easily dismounted the bench. "Thanks for the bagel, Ro. It's been nice to get out of the station for once and enjoy the weather."

"We'll talk to you again soon," I said as I watched her scamper off. Yes, scamper. The energy of youth. She was excited to get out of the office, and I was sitting here uncomfortable from the perspiration running down my back. It's all in the perspective.

CHAPTER 18

"Looks like we've got a full day," Herc said, reaching for his third bagel. "Things starting to come together in that brain of yours?"

"Nothing solid, just possible connections floating around with no homes to land yet."

"Any particular order you want to do this in?"

"Good question. Each one of the five has something in their background that relates to another. It's hard to know where to start and where to end. Plus, we also want to talk to the fiduciary, Helena Sheldon's mother, and Craddock's old girlfriend, Krista Mowbrey. Let's start with a call to Krista Mowbrey but save Helena Sheldon's mother until after we've confronted Helena. I want to confront her without any warning, which her mother might give her."

"I'm with you on that point. I vote for holding off on Bart Sheldon till later. He's so slippery, we need to get as much on him as we can before interviewing him again," Herc said.

That much decided, we agreed to play the rest by ear depending on what we learned from these first contacts and who we then ran into first. I drove my car home with Herc following.

He picked me up from there, and I made the call to Krista Mowbrey on speaker. As it turned out, she still lived in the Orlando area, so we went with interviewing her over the phone. If she dropped a bombshell, we'd meet her in person.

"I don't know what I can tell you about Jed Craddock," she said after we'd done our introductory thing. "It's been months since I saw him."

"Tell us about your relationship with him," I said. "Was it amicable?"

"You mean did we get along? Yes, at first. Jed wasn't a happy guy, so take that into consideration. He wasn't satisfied working in construction. He thought he was meant for bigger things. At first, I liked that. I thought it meant he had ambition and was willing to work to get to whatever goals he set for himself. What I soon learned was that was ego speaking, not dedication. He was looking for the easy way to get to riches and fame."

"Could you give us an example?" Herc asked.

"I assume you're alluding now to the modeling, which is what he was doing when he was killed, right?"

"Right," Herc replied.

"Jed was a free agent in construction. He worked out of an agency, but he was picky about what jobs he took. He didn't like heights, so he stayed away from high rises. I can't blame him there, even though those guys get paid more. Hazard pay, you know? He liked jobs that broke by late afternoon, even though overtime pay would've been good. He didn't like to exert himself more than he had to. Does that help?"

"That's the kind of thing we had in mind," I said.

"There's one more thing. I don't like to speak ill of the dead— well, I guess I already have, telling you about him wanting things the easy way. At least one of his jobs was on the shady side. Those he worked for were skimming off the top of the funds they were drawing down to pay the workers. Jed wanted in on it, not the skimming part, but he thought they'd pay not to have their scheme revealed. Before he approached them, though, the project closed down and he was out of a job."

Was it possible those bosses thought he'd turned them in and had come after him at the studio? Had he been the whistleblower? Even if he wasn't involved that way, Mowbrey had given us another possible motive for his murder, blackmail.

When she ran out of info about Craddock, we thanked her and signed off. "That phone call could send us a totally new direction," I said.

"Looking for our culprit within the construction business?" Herc asked.

"Wouldn't they have found Craddock and gotten their revenge before now? They could've learned his location months ago, especially with Craddock having his own website. And even if they did just learn where he was, wouldn't someone at the studio have noticed an outsider in the building?"

"I thought we decided it would've been easy for someone to slip through one of the less used entrances, make their way to the fitness room, which is centrally located, do the deed and vanish within minutes?"

I blew out a breath. "We're supposed to be zeroing in on the motive and killer. Mowbrey's information has opened up a whole new group of suspects, suspects we can't even pinpoint until we do much more research in construction fraud arrests in the Orlando area."

"I'll put in a call to Oliver and get her started."

"I suppose it wouldn't hurt to be prepared in the event we can't make a case against any of the folks at the studio, but something's telling me that as logical as this construction fraud revenge angle is, it'll only lead us down a blind alley."

Herc called Oliver. "As much as I've come to respect your gut feelings, Ro, I don't want any more time on this one to get away from us," he said after contacting his researcher.

"Krista Mowbrey did shed some new light on the man Craddock was, but in the meantime, let's sharpen our focus on the studio set. Wickersham hasn't mentioned the man's tendency to take the easy way out, including his consideration of blackmail."

"It's a stronger motive for murdering him than his sleeping with Lola."

"Definitely something to keep in mind as we talk to the studio crew again," I said.

THE SHELDON STUDIO HADN'T CHANGED MUCH PHYSICALLY SINCE our last visit, except a pall seemed to linger throughout and a crime scene tape now barred entrance to Craddock's room. Quiet reigned.

We sought out Helena Sheldon first. No brainer. We found her in her office staring at her computer screen. "Not again? Didn't get your fill of harassing me and my people last week?"

Herc was ready for her sarcasm. "Additional information has come to light that has prompted new questions. We've had more time to research your finances. Your business is limping along at best, wouldn't you say, Mrs. Sheldon?"

He was giving her a chance to revise her story on her own. I'd bet money she'd still try to sugarcoat their situation.

She glanced at her computer screen, like she'd find her response there. "Limping along? It's true, business has been off slightly since Jed Craddock's passing, but we'll regroup and rebound in no time at all." Her tone didn't come across quite as hopeful as her words.

Too bad there wasn't real money involved in my bet with myself. I waited for Herc to set her straight. That was one of his real strengths, winnowing a subject down to its real size by hammering the suspect with the evidence.

He started by reciting the amounts in the checking and bank accounts for the studio, her and her husband. "No money has come in for the last month. Your business appears to be dying on the vine. Sorry, I tend to use a lot of cliches."

"It's just a downturn in the business cycle," she said, still trying to bluff her way through Herc's interrogation.

Herc didn't let up. "You're living on your credit cards."

"So?"

"Those bills eventually have to be paid."

"Which we'll do, the same as we have been."

That's what we'd been waiting for. "Yes, you have," Herc said. "Thanks to your daughter's trust fund from her late father's insurance."

She opened her mouth but didn't say anything.

"Yes, we know about that," Herc said. "Our question is, does your daughter know how much you've drained the fund to keep things afloat? Maybe Craddock found out and was blackmailing you to keep her from learning what you were up to?"

She pulled in her lips as she shot from her desk chair. "I don't have to answer your questions. We're all trying to recover from Jed's tragic death, and you won't leave us alone to get our lives back."

"Actually, you do have to answer our questions—now, at the station or under subpoena." Herc's tone had gone full cop.

Neither of us made a move to leave.

My turn. "Does your husband know how much you've spent from the trust fund? How did Craddock find out?"

"Get out," she said, raising her voice.

"We'll be back to get our questions answered," Herc said as he ushered me from the office.

"About what we expected," I said in a lowered voice as we headed for Lola Benson's private quarters. "Notice how she didn't appear to be surprised when you mentioned Craddock and blackmail."

No one had been at the front desk when we arrived. At the time, I'd been surprised the main door was unlocked. Apparently there was still hope for walk-in clients.

"You're back?" Lola said upon opening her door. "You guys stirred up a lot of trouble around here with your last visit. Have you found Jed's killer yet?"

At her invitation, we entered her apartment and took seats in the living room. "No, we haven't learned who murdered the man yet," I replied. "But we're closing in. We've been learning some interesting things about you folks."

"Oh? I thought I was pretty up front when I talked to you. It wasn't fun to admit I'd been sleeping with the guys."

"You did a pretty good job steering us in other directions, Lola, attempting to make us believe either Joel Drysdale or Trey Compton killed Jed Craddock out of jealousy. That was a smart move, except we do our homework and don't tend to take what witnesses tell us at face value. Or believe they've told us the full story."

If possible, she opened her big, brown eyes even wider. "But I did!"

"I don't recall your mentioning the real reason you were asked to leave school, that you'd been caught selling stolen cell phones on campus," I said.

She blinked. "How did you find out?" she asked, surprised. "I thought my mom and Bart paid off some people at the college to bury my case file."

"You're admitting it's true?"

She lowered her head. "Yeah. You don't think I'd have stuck around here this long if my mother and her crook of a husband hadn't intervened and held my mistake over my head ever since?"

"Why did you call your stepfather a crook?" Herc asked.

"Because he is. Anyone can see it by the way he acts."

She'd opened the door on Bart Sheldon. We had to keep pushing. "Crooks aren't identified simply by their appearance. They are people who commit criminal acts," I said.

"Maybe I'm not so good at words. You get the picture, though.

He's a creep. My mother made a huge mistake hooking up with him."

Time for a direct press. "Where did you get the cell phones?"

She flopped into an easy chair, grabbed a throw pillow and placed it in her lap, running her fingers over the fringe in the seams.

"We're not leaving until you tell us," Herc told her.

"You can't do that."

"Maybe not here, but we can take you back to the station and continue to ask you there."

"I should talk to my mother. She'll advise me."

Paydirt! "Just like she's been advising you as administrator of your trust fund?"

"You know about that?"

"We know that your father died suddenly from a construction accident a few years back and that he had a million dollars of life insurance that went into a trust fund for you that you can't get your hands on until you're twenty-one."

"That's right."

"Did you also know that as administrator your mother could tap into the funds?"

"As long as they were spent for my benefit," she said.

"And have you benefited nine hundred thousand dollars' worth? More than that amount, actually," Herc told her.

"Nine … where did you get that figure? I wouldn't still be living in this dump if any real money had been spent on me."

"We just confronted your mother about those expenditures," Herc said. "She refused to answer. But we've got the data. Most of it went to pay for what you call 'this dump.' She's also used it to pay the models and for day-to-day living expenses. Since you're living here, I suppose it's possible she could claim it's all been for you."

She shook her head vehemently. "You must be mistaken. That money is mine. It's the only thing that's kept me going, knowing that soon it will spring me to a whole new life."

She knew we were correct. Tears filled her eyes and were starting to drip down her cheeks. "How could this have happened? I have a fi— someone guarding my trust fund for me."

I really didn't want to be the one to let her know her grandmother had failed her. I chickened out and left that part to Herc. For one who had sold stolen cell phones at one time, she didn't appear to be very bright.

"Your fiduciary is your grandmother. Is that correct?" Herc asked.

She nodded. "Yes. Grandma would never let Mom do that to me."

"Are you sure?" I asked. "How do your mother and grandmother get along?"

"Fine, I guess. They didn't speak for years because of something that happened when my mom was a teen. But they got back together after that."

"And Grandma would do about anything to appease your mother these days to avoid creating another rift," I said.

"At my expense?" She was crying openly now.

"If your mother convinced her everything she was spending was for your benefit?"

Lola thought about my question at length. "Do you folks enjoy bursting folks' bubbles?"

We got that kind of question a lot and usually didn't answer. But this time, I thought it necessary to justify our actions. "Of course we don't, Ms. Benson. But our overriding charge is to find the truth even if that sometimes means making others uncomfortable."

"What did my mother say about having spent so much of my money?"

"She refused to answer," I said.

"You're leaving it up to me to confront her?"

"If you choose," Herc replied.

"But how does this relate to Jed's death? I don't see the connection."

The astuteness of her question surprised me. "We're not sure. Jed could've found out what she was doing and demanded his share to keep quiet."

"And my mother killed him instead?" Her voice rose as the thought sank in.

"It's a possibility," Herc said. "She was the one who found him. She could've just as easily have 'found' him after she murdered him.

"My mother would never do that."

"An hour ago, would you have said she'd be robbing you blind?" I asked.

"No, but I understand that part. Mother isn't good with money because she's never had any. Not that I'm okay with her taking so much from me. But she'd never kill another person. She has trouble killing spiders."

I didn't mention that it had been my experience on occasion that those who couldn't bring themselves to end the life an arachnid could still murder a human. "Have you remembered anything more about Jed Craddock?" I asked.

"I mentioned that he and Bart were having none of each other after Bart walked in on Jed and me, right?"

"Yes?" Herc responded.

"I've remembered that I saw them arguing a day or two before Jed was killed. I didn't hear what they were saying. All I could see from a distance were their gestures. They weren't exactly hugging each other."

"That's all you saw?" Herc asked.

"Yes. Maybe something more will occur to me, but you've given me so much to think about otherwise, I have no idea when my brain will settle down."

"You know how to get in touch with us if you recall anything else," Herc told her.

With that, we left.

Once outside her rooms, I was really anxious to discuss this last interview with Herc, but these corridors, though they appeared deserted, weren't to be trusted.

"Want to go to the car and regroup?" he asked, picking up on my mood.

"Good idea."

We headed for the main entrance.

CHAPTER 19

The last two exchanges called for an energy bar, which I located in my purse, broke in half and shared with Herc. "Is she playing us?" I asked Herc once I finished my half.

Not a real aficionado of energy bars, he still sampled it. "Which one, the mother or the daughter?"

"We know Helena Sheldon is trying to play us without much success, unless she really is a business guru who wants to come across as a classic failure. But I was referring to Lola Benson. I've gone from thinking her a bit of a ditz when we first interviewed her to a Mata Hari type when we supposedly pulled from her that she'd slept with all three men to feeling sorry for her for having a mother who helped herself to Lola's money. Now? I'm not so sure. How could she not know her mother was dipping into her trust fund?"

"Maybe Helena has never taken advantage of her before," Herc replied.

"It's possible, but I'm not buying that theory. Helena didn't become the person we've interviewed overnight. She's spent the better part of her life clawing to the top. She doesn't have the smarts to finish the job, or she wouldn't have had to resort to using her daughter's money."

Herc consumed the last of his half of the bar and shook his head as if wondering why these were so popular. "So far, we've got the goods on Helena being guilty of fraud, and that's only if her daughter chooses to prosecute. That doesn't link her to Craddock's death, unless he found out and threatened to tell Lola or worse, turn her in to the authorities."

"But we learned from Krista Mowbrey that Jed Craddock wasn't above blackmail. It's possible that's what got him killed," I said.

"But why now, when most of the trust fund is gone?"

"He may not have known the extent of Helena's grab, or even if he did, he figured he'd take whatever was left."

Herc sat there thinking for several beats, his fingers drumming the steering wheel. "Okay, let's say Helena Sheldon killed him. How did she pull it off?"

Was this a trick question? We knew most of that possible scenario. "She'd already killed him some time before the meeting was to begin. Then she waited for him to be discovered. When that hadn't happened by the time the meeting was to begin, she decided she'd be the one to find him. When she sent out the search party, she made sure she took the fitness room."

"Okay, you've managed to cover motive and opportunity. What about means?" he asked. I suspected his question was more as devil's advocate than a real challenge to my theory.

"Anyone could've taken the plumber's snake from Wickersham's car, including Helena," I said. "Was she strong enough to use it? Yes, since her victim was at a disadvantage being seated on the stationary bike with his back to the door."

"If we follow that line of thinking, even Lola Benson was capable of killing the guy."

"That's what occurred to me just now as we spoke again with Lola," I said. "Suppose she's a much better actress than we've given her credit for. What if Craddock found out about the state of the trust fund, only instead of going to Helena, he went to Lola and threatened to report her mother to the authorities if Lola didn't pay him off? More than any of the others, Lola could've slipped into the fitness room and done him in without anyone noticing her. She's done her best to convince us she's a nothing in the business, a hanger-on at best."

Herc pulled at an ear. My hypothesis about Lola Benson held enough credibility to compete with the idea of Helena Sheldon murdering Craddock. "Do you really think that young woman is capable of murder?"

"I wouldn't have until we learned she was expelled from school for fencing stolen goods plus the fact she neglected to reveal that piece of her history when we first interviewed her. She claimed she was immature when that happened and that she's grown up, which could be the case, but that act could just as easily have gotten her started along a criminal path. What if she was still fencing? No one pays much attention to her. She could have been coming and going as needed with no one the wiser."

"I never thought we'd be thinking of Lola Benson as a murderer when we started the day," he said.

"But it's all there, Herc. In fact, I didn't even mention the fact that she refused to tell us how she came upon the stolen cell phones. I was hoping she'd implicate her stepfather, but she didn't. Why not? Because there was another source of her goods or because she's either shielding him or is afraid of him? There's more there for us to uncover."

"Why do you do this to me?" he asked, frustration clearly coming through in his tone.

"We both know that's why you want me as your partner, to keep you from going down the wrong path by seizing upon the first theory that works with whatever evidence you've managed to gather at that point."

"But now we've got three possible killers to consider, including Wickersham, and we haven't even talked again with the men."

"By now, Helena or maybe even Lola will have tipped off Bart Sheldon that we're digging deeper and are already aware of more evidence against them than they thought possible. We probably should get to him next," I said.

"Even though we don't have enough on him yet?"

"The longer we wait, the more time he'll have to cover his tracks, wherever they lead."

"You're right. We've been in this situation before and bluffed our way through," he replied. "Guess we could give it a shot now."

"There's no law or principle of law enforcement that says we only get two times at bat," I said. "We let him think we know more than we do. Who knows what he'll do in response?"

"Then let's get to it while I'm fired up."

CHAPTER 20

Once again, we found Bart Sheldon lounging at the pool. No newspaper this time, but a glass of dark liquid was positioned quite near him. Whiskey, most likely, and a double shot. Sunbathing, his hairy oversize body was swathed in suntan lotion.

He raised his sunglasses as we approached. "Heard I could be expecting a visit from the two of you. Just so you know, I don't have anything else to add. I was a mere secondary player in that murder scene, showing up after the others to lend assistance, which wasn't needed, other than to calm my wife."

As Herc and I pulled up deck chairs on both sides of him, I tossed a beach towel his direction. "Wouldn't want you to burn while we talk. And don't concern yourself that interviewing you again is a waste of our time. We've been gathering more background information than was at our disposal when we talked to you before and have some additional questions. A few things to clarify."

He arranged the towel across his torso, leaving his lower parts still exposed to the sun's rays. "How thoughtful. All right. Fire away. Although the sun's pretty warm today. How long can you both tolerate the heat?"

"Don't worry about us, Sheldon," Herc said, assuming his best commanding tone. "This shouldn't take long. Like Mrs. Summerfield said, we just want to follow up on a few items."

"Have at it," Sheldon said, his voice as oily as ever.

"We understand you and Helena Benson were married four years ago," I said.

"Yes. Good one. Very penetrating."

"A few years later, you started this studio. Is that correct?"

"Yes."

"What did you do before that?"

"What? You don't have my employment record?"

"Answer the question, Mr. Sheldon," Herc said in his most official tone.

Before answering, Sheldon took a sip from his glass. "I've been in some form of agricultural management my entire career until I met Helena a few years back when we got interested in the modeling industry."

Even now, most likely knowing we knew all about his employment history, he still portrayed his background in general, glowing terms. "That's quite a leap," I said. "How did you go from agricultural management to owning a modeling agency? Did you or your wife ever model yourselves?"

He snorted. "Neither of us has what you'd call the physique for modeling. Helena was in the entertainment industry, where she met several celebrities, amongst them a few models. I hit it off with one of those contacts, a guy named Zane Billings. He'd been a model himself years before but when we met, he was operating his own small agency after acting as a modeling agent a while."

Interesting how he'd circumnavigated the question without actually answering it. I tried again. "What made the two of you decide to open your own agency?"

"She had a boss who was a real tyrant. Wanted her to work extra hours without paying her. And the farm implements business, which I was in, was becoming more computerized. One night when we were having dinner with Billings and complaining about our jobs, he suggested we consider opening our own modeling agency."

"That took a major financial investment," Herc said, deciding it was time to go for the jugular. "Where'd you get the money?"

"Can't help you there. That is confidential information."

"It's not a matter of 'helping' us, Sheldon. This is an official police investigation. If you won't tell us here, we'll get a warrant."

"Go ahead. Be my guest."

"Did the money come from your private business?" I asked, ignoring his challenge.

He cocked his head and stared at me through hooded lids. "Private business?" He laughed. "This studio is my business. My only business."

"What about the stolen goods you house from time to time?" Herc asked.

"Sorry. The stories of my participation in that business are pure fabrication of police and feds attempting to muddy my name. Check your records, if you haven't already. No claims of my dealing in stolen goods have ever stuck."

I stood there willing his smug self-confidence to roll off me. From Herc's firm jaw, I could tell he was experiencing the same urge.

I let Herc handle the next part. "Perhaps the money came from elsewhere. A pot of money that has been at your disposal through Helena and seemingly could be used legally."

Sheldon blinked once, twice, and his chin revealed a tic. "I have no idea what you're talking about."

"No? Well, not to worry. We won't bother you further about it. You can't control it anyhow."

Herc nodded, and the two of us abandoned our chairs in unison.

"That was a huge risk," I said as soon as we were out of Bart Sheldon's hearing. "He thinks we haven't got the goods on him."

"Well, we haven't," Herc replied.

"True. But just as his self-confidence increased back there, you brought up Lola's trust fund without naming it. If he hasn't heard from Helena about it yet, he soon will know we're on to that scheme. But he doesn't know what we plan to do about it. That's the crack we wanted to jam into that self-satisfaction. Now we wait and let it fester."

NEXT UP WAS JOEL DRYSDALE, SINCE WE RAN INTO HIM WHEN WE emerged into the lobby.

"No, I did not kill Jed Craddock," he said upon noticing us. "That's all you need to know from me."

"Even if that's the case, Mr. Drysdale," I said, approaching him, "you may be able to help us zero in on the real culprit. Is there somewhere private we can talk?"

He scowled but just briefly. I got the impression he wasn't as recalcitrant as he wanted to appear. He was playing to whoever else might be listening, which suggested the man was trying to still hang on to whatever future he might have with the studio.

He led us back to the training room, where we all took a seat.

"Are you any closer to finding out who murdered Jed?" he asked before we had a chance to launch into our questions.

"We've learned a lot more about everyone here at the studio since we last talked. We want to build on that knowledge today," Herc replied without answering his question directly. "Have you remembered anything else about Craddock, your relationship with him or any of the events leading up to his death?"

Drysdale leaned forward. "I've been thinking back on those days before we found him in the fitness room. Something happened between that Thursday when the five of us spent part of Thanksgiving together and that Tuesday night."

This was the first we'd heard about Thanksgiving. "What five of you?" I asked, since there were six people living here before the murder.

"Craddock, his girlfriend, Compton, Lola and me."

"Who are you referring to as Craddock's girlfriend?"

"Harper. I don't recall her last name."

"Wickersham," Herc said. "Tell us more about that day. Were you all here or somewhere else?"

"The group chipped in for a turkey dinner with all the fixings that she, uh, Harper, picked up on her way to the studio. We ate in Lola's apartment and after that watched a football game. We weren't like a bunch of lifetime friends getting together, but it was the holiday and some of us, mainly Lola, wanted to follow tradition."

"Helena and Bart Sheldon didn't attend?" I asked.

"No. Lola said they were taking her grandmother out to a restaurant and hadn't invited her, so she wanted to do something with the rest of us so she didn't sit in her apartment alone."

"How long were you all there?" Herc asked.

"Till about five or so. When the game ended. Lola wanted us to stick around and have turkey sandwiches with her, but Harper begged off. Said she'd had enough football and left. Compton rubbed his stomach, still flat as ever, and declared it nap time. I wasn't crazy about sitting around making small talk with just Lola and Craddock, but the offer of an old-fashioned turkey sandwich complete with cranberry sauce was too tempting to refuse. When we found another ball game to watch, Lola begged off and went to the kitchen to pack up leftovers."

Drysdale had spent time alone with Craddock that day. There could be more there than we already knew. "That was Thursday. You said something must've happened between then and Tuesday. Why do you say that?" I asked.

He wrinkled his nose. "We went from having a fairly good time together on Thursday and five days later, one of us was gone."

"But Helena and Bart Sheldon weren't present for your Thanksgiving get-together," I said. "Maybe the 'something' you mention happened because of them?"

"Well, there was that hastily called meeting Tuesday night.

Something prompted it. If I were to guess, I'd say one or both of them learned in that time that the business couldn't go on the way it was. But I'm just speculating. They didn't explain then and they haven't said since the murder what's going on."

"Does that mean the studio is still open to business?" Herc asked.

"Beats me. We haven't been told anything officially, but we haven't been kicked out. Compton had one job late last week, so it's not like the place is completely shut down."

"Have you been looking for a new position?" I asked.

"In this business, you're always looking, but no, my plan for the moment is to stick around here and see what happens. Now that there's just two of us, my chances of more employment have risen. In my opinion, neither Helena nor Bart are very good managers, and that's what the business needs. That and someone with better connections."

"Someone like you?" Herc asked.

Drysdale chuckled. "Since you bring it up, yeah. That hasn't been my plan, although I have played with the idea from time to time."

Since he'd relaxed somewhat, time to ask the tough question. "Did Craddock learn the real reason why you left the Margaret Kane Agency in Miami?" I asked.

Although he didn't flinch, his right hand went to the collar of his knit shirt. "Real reason? I'm not sure what you mean. I left to go out on my own."

"True, but only after your reputation dipped after an incident in which you were charged with making off with a client's products."

His hand remained at his collar, pulling it away from his neck. "The charges were dropped. It was never proven."

"But there was enough doubt that after you continued to lose jobs, it was strongly suggested you go out on your own," I said. "If Craddock had come across that information, he could've used it to have you fired from the Sheldon Studio. Would that account for the low balance in your bank account? There've been a lot of cash withdrawals of fifty or seven-five dollars at a time. Were those payouts to him?"

He sat back in his chair, his expression becoming firmer. "Wow. Not only have you been digging around in my past, which I get—that's your job—you've taken what I just told you and invented a passable motive for my killing him. But that's all it was, your invention."

Neither Herc nor I spoke. We waited for him to get past his anger and answer.

"Are you that desperate to find the person responsible you'd make up a story like that?"

We waited some more. Silence is sometimes the most compelling way to finesse a confession.

"I get it. You think your silence will get me to talk. Well, sorry. As far as I know, Craddock didn't have any information about my background, or if he did, he didn't threaten to use it against me. I play the ponies. Okay? Stupid, I know, because I rarely win. Just enough to keep me handing over a few bucks every so often."

His reason sounded legit. But Herc wasn't quite ready to thank him for his information and move on. "Did Craddock ever threaten to blackmail you about anything else?"

That stopped the male model momentarily. He clasped his hands together and rested his jaw on them. "Funny you should ask about blackmail. We did relax our defenses while we drank and watched the game. He brought up a shady construction job he'd worked and how he'd had the goods on the skimming his bosses were doing on the side and would've made a small fortune cashing in on what he knew had the authorities not closed in. I said something like, 'You mean blackmail?' and he backed off and told me he hadn't meant exactly that. When I asked what he had meant, he changed the subject." He unclasped his hands and gazed directly at us. "If you were asking if I thought he was capable of blackmail, based on that conversation, I'd say yes. In fact ..."

"Yes?" I asked.

"During commercials, we'd share bits and pieces about our backgrounds. In all the months we'd worked here, that was the first time our exchange was more than superficial. Competing for the same jobs can do that to a person. You don't want to give the other guys any leg up they can use against you. Anyway, at one point he asked me what I really thought of Bart Sheldon. I replied that the guy was a jerk, and from what I could tell, he did nothing more to keep the business going than show up for an occasional 'lecture,' which was a joke. The guy hardly knew anything about the business. But I didn't plan to cross him because he'd go right to Helena."

"How did Craddock respond to that?" Herc asked, apparently like me realizing we'd uncovered some new ground.

"He suggested Sheldon wasn't invulnerable. When I asked what he knew about the man, he got real cagey, like he wanted to tell me more to lord it over me that he knew something I didn't, and he did get close to saying something, but then he backed away. When I pushed to know more, he told me to open my eyes. There was more going on with Bart Sheldon than I realized."

"And?" Herc asked.

"That's what I was getting at. What I just did to you, he did to me. Got me interested and then backed off before he said too much. Only I backed away because I don't know anything more."

"Nothing else has occurred to you since then?" I asked. "There's been time since you talked to him for you to replay what went on between the two of you that evening given what happened to him five days later."

"He told me to open my eyes, which is what I've been trying to do. Who wouldn't anyway, with a murder to think about? Everyone's made themselves scarce since then, little hanging out together. But before then, I kept an eye on Sheldon as much as I could. Since I'd avoided him in the past, I was surprised how much about his personality I'd missed." He held up a hand as if to rephrase. "Not so much his personality. What I mean are his actions.

"The guy is shifty. I knew that before, but he's always looking over his shoulder. I didn't figure out why. He likes to make a show of lounging out at the pool. Never goes in. What I hadn't realized was how close that area is to the back pool entrance, which leads directly to one of the first-floor rooms. Once, I observed him opening that room with a key. Another time, I saw him coming out of that same room. He didn't just leave; he looked all around him before moving away."

"I don't suppose you tried to check out that room once he was gone?" Herc asked.

"I tried, but I couldn't find a key that fit."

"That it?" Herc again.

"Late Sunday night, early Monday morning, I thought I heard something in one of the rooms below mine, but when I went outside to investigate, I couldn't see anything, although I thought I heard a vehicle starting up and driving away. I might've heard footsteps running away, but I couldn't be sure. When I checked again Monday morning, there was no evidence of whatever it had been but must've been something because it awakened me from deep sleep."

I took a few seconds to process his words. "Earlier, you said you thought something had happened between Thanksgiving and Tuesday night. Would those late-night sounds qualify?" I asked.

He shrugged. "Maybe. If it wasn't just my imagination messing with me. I hadn't even thought about these things, watching Sheldon, hearing noises, until you started quizzing me again."

"You've still got my card, don't you?" Herc asked.

Drysdale nodded.

Herc handed him another. "Just in case you can't find the other one. If you recall anything more, give me a call."

"You think Sheldon's got more to do with Jed's death than it has appeared?"

"Maybe. Right now, we're following up any lead that looks possible," Herc replied. "In the meantime, don't share what you've told us with anyone. And if the walls start closing in and you feel you're in danger, call immediately."

"Yeah, sure," Drysdale said, not sounding convinced.

"We mean it, man," Herc said in the most serious tone I'd heard from him yet.

We thanked Drysdale and went in search of Trey Compton.

CHAPTER 21

We discovered the other surviving male model in the fitness room, despite the crime scene tape we'd left in place.

"When you gonna take the tape down?" he asked Herc.

"You didn't pay attention to it anyhow," Herc replied. "We're keeping it up while this investigation is still underway, just in case there might be some evidence still here we haven't found."

"Gonna kick me out?"

"You're here now. In exchange, we want more information."

"I don't know much more I can tell you," Compton replied, resuming his work with the free weights.

"Let us be the judge of that," I said. "Tell us about Thanksgiving."

He put the weights down. "What's that got to do with Craddock's murder?"

"We understand it was the last time the three of you were together, along with Lola Benson and Craddock's girlfriend, Harper Wickersham. It was also the first time in months, if ever, that you all relaxed and enjoyed each other's company. Tell us about that. What did you talk about?" I asked.

He appeared to be surprised at my question. "You want me to remember conversations that far back?"

"Not word for word. Just the gist of your chat."

"You're serious, aren't you? This isn't a question just to be asking a question."

Was he stalling? "That's right."

He stroked his jaw. "Joel and I got there first. Around one. Jed arrived next, and his girlfriend showed up with the food about ten minutes later. Although we'd all chipped in for the turkey dinner she'd picked up on her way, she acted like it was her treat. Whatever, no one else had volunteered to get it. It was all ready to eat, so we spent the next few minutes laying everything out on the counter, then we helped ourselves and sat at the table Lola had set. That the kind of thing you wanted?"

"Yes," I replied. "Once you were all seated, what did you talk about while you ate?"

"As it turned out, to everyone's surprise but Lola, we'd been looking forward to this get-together. Not so much the company but the food. Usually, the three of us guys have to watch what we eat, but not on Thanksgiving. We didn't really talk a lot at first. We were all too busy stuffing ourselves and getting our fill of the bird, the stuffing and mashed potatoes before the others got it all. After that, we started to reminisce about past Thanksgivings. All except Lola. She remained pretty silent. Funny how a stupid holiday can make three grown men act like oldsters thinking back on the 'good old days.'"

Herc was growing impatient to move on. "And after lunch, we understand you all watched a football game. What did you talk about then?"

"Football, of course. We watched two pro teams go at it. There was some talk about betting, but in the end, we skipped that part. Our pay has been pretty sparse lately. So we switched to taking a sip of our beers with each score. That didn't last long. It was a defensive game, pretty boring. While we drank, we talked about our bosses. Lola started it, saying how glad she was Helena and

Bart had taken her grandmother out for dinner. Knowing her grandmother, she would probably make them stay at her house for extra pumpkin pie well into the afternoon. Lola was still smoldering from Bart's interrupting her and Craddock going at it, even though she knew full well that's what caused our fight. She apparently assumed the three of us had made up and all three of us still adored her."

"And that wasn't the case?" I asked, also wanting to move him along now that he'd gotten to the juicy part.

"Not completely. We were getting along that day because we were enjoying the holiday, a welcome change from what has become an extremely boring existence. Plus, Harper was there. From the surprised expression on her face, it was obvious she hadn't known about Lola and Craddock. She stuck around a little longer, pretended to watch the game, but she didn't drink much and stayed in a corner. Like I told you, she left without Craddock."

"You said Lola wanted to talk about her mother and stepfather," Herc said. "How did that discussion go?"

"Slowly at first. None of us could be sure she wouldn't report whatever we said to Helena and Bart. To gain our trust, she began by telling us things about the two of them. How her mother tried to get into the modeling business herself by sleeping with a number of TV and radio execs and failed miserably. How Bart Sheldon had been working for a Miami kingpin when her mother met him. Lola wasn't sure what he'd been doing, but every so often he'd leave her mother in the middle of the night to attend to business for his boss. She'd hear her mother begging him not to go and Bart reassuring her he'd be back soon. Once, Lola had come upon some of the guy's bloodied clothes in the garbage that hadn't been disposed of yet. When she asked her mother what had happened, she was told to forget it and never mention it to anyone, especially Bart."

"How did the rest of you react to her revelations?" I asked.

"We were stunned at first. No one drank for several minutes.

Drysdale asked if she or any of us knew how much of a cut Sheldon was getting from the business. Lola didn't know. Craddock shared that he'd overheard an argument between the two Sheldons a while back. He couldn't hear much of it, but he thought he'd heard her accuse him of doing nothing to earn his ten percent of each booking. Drysdale and I exchanged looks. We were only getting thirty percent ourselves. That meant Helena was taking in sixty percent. Only a small part of that had to be going to administrative costs. I took cold comfort from realizing the three of us must be receiving the same cut."

Craddock appeared to do a lot of eavesdropping. Was that what had gotten him killed? "How about you?" I asked. "Did you share any information with the others?"

"By this time, I'd had quite a bit to drink. It wasn't like I had to drive home, just make it up the stairs to my room. I was well aware that I was getting most of the bookings, which wasn't going over well with the other two guys. You've probably heard how the two of them beat me up just a week or so before. Ironically, that seemed to clear the air, at least enough for us to get along okay on Thanksgiving.

"In my beer-soaked brain, I decided they might give me a break if they knew the price I was paying, so I told them about Helena's demands. Not everything. Too embarrassing, and should I ever make it in this business, I wouldn't want the worst parts to get out. I limited my disclosure to having to paint her toenails and drink champagne from one of her shoes. Do you know how disgusting that was? But it bought me some good will with the other two."

"What about Bart Sheldon? Did you or the other two have anything more to say about him?" Herc asked.

"Craddock started to say something at one time, but his girl-friend dragged him out to the lobby. He returned alone, saying Wickersham had opted to go home. She claimed she'd eaten too much and had a stomachache. Once he was back, he must've forgotten what he'd been about to say about good ole Bart. I stayed a little longer, then the beer started to get to me, so I left. If anything else was said about Sheldon, I don't know."

I eyed Herc. He nodded. We'd gotten about as much as we could from Compton for now. Coupled with what we'd learned from Drysdale, we'd gleaned quite a bit this time around.

"What are your plans, Mr. Compton?" Herc asked.

"I'm sticking around for a while. I got a booking last week. Maybe there'll be more."

Herc gave Compton a second card as he'd done with Drysdale.

As we were leaving the fitness room, we heard loud voices down the hall. We took off to investigate.

As it turned out, Lola was in her mother's office doing the shouting. We stopped short of the door and listened. "I'll never forgive you for this, Mother. I trusted you, and look what you've done to my nest egg."

"Can't you see, Lola? It was an investment in your future. We may have hit a rocky spot, but we can recover from this."

"With what? There's hardly any money coming in and very little left of my trust fund. I can't believe Grandma let this happen."

"She wants the same for you. That's why she's been willing to trust me to build this business."

"You still don't get it." Lola was now shouting. "There no longer is a business. And on top of that, we've got Jed's murder making things worse. What's your creep of a husband doing to help? He's still making money with his side hustle. Why hasn't he put some of that into this business?"

"What side hustle? Bart's been spending all his time trying to get this business off the ground."

"Open your eyes, Mother. That man never left his Miami ties behind."

"I know you've never cared for him. I've been able to live with that. But to accuse him of being a criminal is totally unfounded. You can't repeat that to anyone, especially with the police breathing down our necks."

I glanced at Herc, and he nodded. That was our cue.

"Speaking of the police ..." Herc said, bursting in on them. I followed behind him.

With our arrival, Helena Sheldon went on the offensive. "You're the ones who told her about her trust fund, aren't you?" She didn't give us chance to answer. "The state of our finances is none of your business. I planned to tell my daughter about her trust fund in my own way, at a time of my own choosing."

"How could you have possibly explained your treating yourself to nearly all the money in the trust fund in a way that wouldn't anger me?" Lola Benson screamed, leaning into her mother's face. "There's no way around the fact that you robbed me."

Helena Sheldon sent Herc and me a look intended to freeze us in our tracks, but we had no intention of leaving this mother-daughter quarrel just yet. She had no recourse but to attempt to justify her actions in front of us. "I did this all for you, darling. I've had to fight and scramble for everything I've ever gotten. I didn't want that kind of life for you. This agency will do that. It's just that we're still in the growing stage. We have more to do. You just need to be patient and let me make this come alive for you."

I couldn't believe this was happening. Helena had been caught red-handed stealing her daughter's money, and she had the gall to claim it was all done for Lola's benefit. But this was Lola Benson's call. After all, this was her mother, who could potentially go to jail if Lola went to the authorities. But if she didn't stand up to the woman now, she ran the risk of being forever under her hand.

Herc and I waited for one of them to say or do something. We were getting so close to uncovering our murderer, we didn't want the moment to pass without taking advantage of it.

Lola turned to us. "Would you mind waiting for me outside? I have some unfinished business with my mother."

"We'll be right outside. Call if you need us," Herc told her.

"We stirred up quite a ruckus in there," Herc said as we made our way down the hall outside Helena Sheldon's office.

We didn't go far. We both sensed some sort of break was coming. "If I read Lola right back there, she wants to work with us more than she has already. We don't want to miss this opportunity."

Herc shook his head in disgust. "That's some mother she's got. No apologies or denials. Instead, she's the hero coming to rescue her daughter from living in poverty."

"Lola saw through it, though," I said. "The question is, will she tolerate it?"

We didn't have to wait long. We could hear the sound of heavy crying, no, wailing, coming from the open door. Lola emerged, her expression tough and defiant.

"After your visit, I went to see an attorney to find out what I should do. I learned I can sue my mother, and my grandmother, for that matter, for the amount of what has been taken from the fund, but realistically, I don't think I'd see any of that money. But I can also make claim to any of the physical property purchased with my money, even though everything's probably in her name. I just hope she didn't put things in both their names."

"I'm not an attorney," I said, "but most likely, she's guilty of fraud."

"I'm letting my attorney handle that. Just now, I demanded to see the books and the password to the accounts. I'm not very good at math, but with my attorney's help and possibly by hiring an accountant, we might be able to save me from this insanity."

"That's good," Herc told her. "Do you plan to open the place up as a motel again?"

"I, uh, haven't the slightest idea yet. But I had to take a stand. I couldn't let her continue to take my money."

"No, of course not," I told her. "I hope you understand. It was important for our investigation for us to learn if you knew what your mother has been up to." It wasn't an apology. That wasn't in the cards from our professional standpoint, but we needed to say something. Besides, we seemed to have done her a service. We were witnessing a transformation from irresponsible ingenue to actual adult.

"It was rude but exactly what I needed to hear. I've been floundering here as my mother's boarder, so bored I'd go to bed with the guys. Boarder, bored, I made a pun." She laughed at her own humor. "The guys have been like brothers to me until I, uh, you know? Now, well, until you guys figure out who murdered Jed, I'm in a sort of holding pattern. At least I'll have the studio's books to keep me company."

I was ready to give her the name of my accountant and caught myself at the last minute. Not professional. Nor smart, because we had to keep our lives separate from suspects' lives while a case was still active. "Good luck," I said. That kind of thing was allowed.

She'd been about to move on but pulled up. "I got them from Bart."

"What?" Apparently this new Lola hadn't completely left the spacey one behind.

"The cell phones I sold on the sly on campus. The month before I left for school, I discovered his stash. Right here at the studio. It's no wonder they haven't taken on more models. He's been using the extra rooms to store his goodies. I didn't think he'd miss one box, and I was strapped for cash. They'd paid for my tuition and room and board, probably out of my trust fund, but I had to earn my own spending money. Rather than get a job, I took the easy way out. And you know the rest. Anyway, thanks for setting me straight about the trust fund."

"Did you hear what I heard?" I asked Herc as we watched her stride down the hall, a new bounce in her gait.

"You mean the part about Sheldon stockpiling his loot here?"

"After all this, she just laid it out there for us to run with," I said, still in a state of shock.

"Don't get carried away yet," he said. "We have confirmation Bart Sheldon used this place as a storehouse at one time. We still don't know those were stolen goods, and even if they were, is he still dealing? We'd have to catch him with the goods to make any charges stick. And even if we could do that, how would his dealing relate to the murder?"

"Spoilsport. You couldn't give me a moment to enjoy this tiny advance in the case."

"You know the rules as well as I, Ro. We don't let ourselves jump to conclusions until all the parts fit."

My shoulders slumped. Involuntarily. My body accepted the "rules" before my brain caught up. "You're right. We know we're on the right path. We just have to prove it."

"Got any ideas how?" he asked.

"Let's go back to my place and lay this out on the white boards."

CHAPTER 22

We picked up cheeseburgers, fries and sodas on the way and brought them back to my duplex to devour them. We both had developed enormous appetites from our second round of questioning the folks at the studio. Plus, celebration of our latest piece of information, Lola Benson's mention of Bart Sheldon's secret hideaway for his cell phones, seemed to be in order.

Since Herc had joined me, I didn't expect Jason to make an appearance anytime soon. I'd have to wait until after Herc left to see how soon my boy showed up.

"Why don't you list the suspects in the order in which we interviewed them," Herc said. "Then we'll cull the most important nuggets that have a direct bearing on this case."

I was still somewhat bummed that, even though Lola Benson had revealed something we hadn't expected to hear, it didn't provide the evidence we needed. If our goal now was to focus only on whatever hard evidence we had or still needed, Herc's plan was as good as any. "Okay, we'll try it your way."

Bart Sheldon—Told us nothing, refused to say how he and Helena had financed the studio and denied any part in dealing stolen goods. No direct tie between Lola's admission she'd pilfered cell phones she'd found on the property to Sheldon except her word, and she hates him. Appeared to let down his guard when the trust fund was brought up; didn't seem to know Helena had been stealing from it.

"Don't forget about that guy who got them interested in running a modeling agency, Zane Billings," Herc said when I'd finished.

"Do you think we need to talk to him? He's probably still in Miami."

"Sheldon didn't really answer our question about how they got interested. Even if it has no bearing on this case, I'd like to know why these two amateurs made the switch. There had to be other ways they could make a buck. Easier and less expensive ways."

We moved on to Joel Drysdale.

Joel Drysdale—Told us Craddock had considered blackmail at least once, but that was his word, again, no hard evidence. Blackmail does suggest motive. Denied the withdrawals from his bank account were to Craddock, who might've learned of the incident at Miami modeling agency. Craddock told Drysdale to keep his eyes open around Bart Sheldon; again, only Drysdale's word. Drysdale thought he heard noises in middle of the night before Craddock's death; still, only his word.

"Hadn't realized how much the guy insinuated and how little evidence there was to back him up until we reduced our interview with him to just a few points," Herc said.

"Even if the blackmail theory is correct," I said, "who would Craddock have been aiming at? Bart Sheldon's the best candidate, but there's also Helena Sheldon, if he found out about the trust fund; Drysdale, if there was more to that incident with the client's missing products; or Compton, if Craddock had learned more disgusting details about Helena's demands on him."

"You didn't mention Lola Benson. Nothing there?"

I stopped and considered my reply. "I wouldn't dismiss her entirely, but she's moved down my list of likely suspects."

"But Drysdale did tell us how the five of them had spent Thanksgiving together. No one mentioned it until then. Also, he told us Wickersham apparently hadn't known about Craddock's sleeping with Lola until that day. Since she left without Craddock after speaking with him privately, there may be more to their breakup than she told us."

"Time to interview Ms. Wickersham again."

I nodded. Harper Wickersham could have and should have told us about the Thanksgiving get-together.

Trey Compton—Seems recovered from Craddock and Drysdale's beating but could be an act. Enough of a motive to kill Craddock? Trouble in high school doesn't seem worth blackmail, although whatever he was forced to do for Helena might be.

Helena and Lola—When confronted about the trust fund, Helena attempted to explain that she'd been using money from the trust fund for Lola's benefit; Lola didn't buy it.

Lola—Consulted attorney about missing money. She will take possession of the building. Got the cell phones to sell on campus from raiding Bart Sheldon's stock, but only her word.

"That's quite a list," Herc said when I finished. "Too much. How do we streamline it?"

"First, we tie up the loose ends, at least with this Billings guy in Miami, and then we talk to Wickersham again."

He frowned, one of his tells for agreeing with whatever I'd proposed but not being satisfied. "Sure, why not. Maybe one of them will tell us something that will nail down the motive. We still don't know anything for sure other than the time of death, the murder weapon and who all found him."

WE DIDN'T FIND A PHONE LISTING FOR A BILLINGS MODELING Agency in the Miami area or the rest of the state. But there was a Z. Billings listed in West Palm Beach, so we tried it. It rang four times before it was answered.

"Yeah?" a growly voice on the other end said.

Herc took this one. I stayed on speaker. "We understand you knew a guy by the name of Bart Sheldon at one time. Is that correct?" he asked after ensuring this was the right guy and introducing us.

"I might have. Why?"

"Is it true you got his wife and him interested in opening their own modeling agency?"

"They really went through with it? I told him they didn't have a snowball in Florida's chance of making it. But then he lost his job and she quit hers and we lost touch when they moved to central Florida. That's all I know."

"Why didn't you think they could make a go of it?" I asked.

"You've met them, right?"

"Yes, but we asked you," I replied.

"It's not like I was friends with either. Neither is very smart and Bart is lazy. He got fired from selling farm machinery because he couldn't or wouldn't learn how to operate the computers that equipment now required. They saw me running my own modeling agency and thought it was the good life. They wanted a piece of it, no matter how many times I told them how much work it was and how much financing they would need not just to get it off the ground but to keep it going."

"How about you?" Herc asked. "It doesn't appear you're still running your own agency."

"Shoulda taken my own advice. You gotta keep getting the

bookings. That works as long as you've got a deep stable of bank-able models, but once they start gaining a name for themselves, they're out the door with fat new contracts from larger agencies. I couldn't keep up. Fortunately, I've been able to make a lot of friends over the years, friends with deep pockets who keep me employed as a consultant."

"What do you know about Bart Sheldon's connection to orga-nized crime?" Herc asked.

"I wouldn't be surprised, but I don't know anything."

Herc didn't give up. "How about trafficking in stolen goods?"

"Again, nothing. But I'd be more likely to believe that than a connection to organized crime. Like I said, the guy's lazy. If he found a way to avoid the stealing or the selling part, like simply passing them along, yeah, he'd jump right on that."

Billings was confirming what we'd been told and observed for ourselves about Bart Sheldon, but he hadn't given us anything new. "Anything else you can tell us about either Helena or Bart Sheldon?" I asked.

Radio silence for a couple of beats. "You can probably tell I didn't like the guy. Didn't trust him. He saw me as having made it financially, which was far from the truth, and glommed onto me. Showed up uninvited more than once. Every so often he'd have money to burn, even after he lost his job. I asked him more than once how he'd acquired his little pot of gold, and he sloughed me off. Told me I didn't want to know."

"Any idea what he meant by that?" I asked.

"Only that he wasn't coming by it legitimately, but he was right. I didn't want to know. For such things like that. Plausible deniability, I think they call it."

"Should anything else occur to you that you do feel like shar-ing," Herc told him, "give us a call."

"Was that as disappointing for you as it was for me?" I asked Herc once he'd hung up.

"Not completely. Up until now, other than what Oliver has been able to gather for us, all we knew about Bart Sheldon has

been what we've heard from Wickersham and the other inhabi-
tants of the studio. Billings was a voice from the past. He
confirmed Sheldon was just as disgusting then as he is now. Leop-
ards and spots, you know?"

"You're right. Just no hard evidence."

"Still, the guy's come up a notch or two on my list of most
likely killers," he said. "Let's go see if Wickersham can add more."

CHAPTER 23

efore we left my place to head to the Mehaffy project, I set out just a couple of Jason's favorite treats. Of course he hadn't appeared while Herc had been here. I hadn't expected anything more. Meeting up with Wickersham again shouldn't take long, then I'd be back for the evening. We'd see then how long he stayed away.

Wickersham was just finishing up for the day when we arrived at the project. "Are you here to check on the house or to tell me you've found Jed's killer?" she asked as soon as she saw me.

"Actually, Lieutenant Morgan and I have a few more questions for you. Is there someplace around here we can talk in private?" I said.

"It'll have to be your car. My truck's full of equipment."

I did a quick review of the state of Herc's car. Hopefully we'd cleaned out all the fast food bags, candy bar wrappers and coffee containers. She climbed into the back seat, and we took our usual seats in the front. Not the most conducive seating arrangement for a follow-up interview but the best option at the moment.

"We learned some new information from the occupants of the studio that we want to run by you," I said by way of introduction. "Why didn't you tell us what happened on Thanksgiving?"

She put her hand to her mouth. "Oh. I guess I forgot to mention that when we've spoken before. Was it important?"

"You gave us the impression that you hadn't spent time at the studio recently. And that you hadn't been getting along with anyone there. We heard a different story," I said.

"I didn't enjoy myself much that day, but who wants to be on their own on Thanksgiving?"

"We also learned that was the first time you heard about Craddock sleeping with Lola Benson. Is that the case?"

She let out a frustrated breath. "Okay, that's right."

"And shortly thereafter you left," Herc said.

"Yes, a big turkey dinner and a couple football games was all I could take of the togetherness. Since I'd driven and Jed had been drinking all afternoon, I took off on my own."

I twisted around to gaze at her more directly. "Time to come clean, Harper. That's the reason why the two of you split up. The two of you left the Benson woman's apartment and he returned several minutes later without you. Is that when it happened? And you were the one to do it. Not him, like you told us."

She bit a lip and studied her hands. A much longer inspection than necessary. She took her time responding. "I wasn't hurt by his unfaithfulness. We'd been on the verge of breaking up for some time. I was just embarrassed that the others all seemed to know about it and I had to find out about it that afternoon. But I didn't completely end things when we were outside in the hall. I told him I needed some space to get past what I'd heard. He appeared to go along with that, so I didn't see him the rest of the weekend. Then Monday he called and begged me to go out to dinner that evening to discuss things."

"This is where we came in originally," Herc said. "Except then you told us he was the one who broke things off, and now we know you were the wronged party. What happened to change things?"

"I wish I could say, although thinking back on that dinner, I should've known what was coming. He was withdrawn. Edgy.

Something was definitely on his mind. At the time, I didn't notice because I was still smarting from learning about him and Lola. I agreed to dinner to test myself. To see if being with him again was enough to change my mind, to forgive him. Funny, I was just coming around to that point when he said he thought it best we break things off."

"Out of the blue?" I asked. "You had no inkling that was coming?"

"No. In retrospect, I should've suspected something. "Since then, I've been so focused on being cheated out of the chance to end things, I haven't really thought about the rest of that dinner until now."

Craddock's changed feelings could be connected to his death. On the other hand, we still didn't have a very good understanding of who the man was. He simply could've been cutting his losses before Wickersham did. On the off chance his actions were related to someone murdering him, we had to keep pushing Wickersham. She might know something she didn't realize she knew. "Now that you're thinking back on that night, does anything else occur to you that you've overlooked until now?"

"At first, everything seemed to be going well, although that was probably because there'd been no mention of what happened on Thanksgiving or even our relationship before that day. Just small talk. I guess I relaxed and started to remember how good things had been between the two of us. I must've said something about moving on. I'm sure it wasn't about forgiving him. I wasn't ready to go there yet. But his tone and manner changed. He backed his chair away from the table. 'I can't go on like this, Harper. You've been a nice diversion, but I need all my energy for my career. Have a good life.' He raised his voice as he said it. 'I don't want to see you again,' he added, standing. I realize now he was deliberately drawing attention to us."

"Why do you think that was?" Herc asked.

She sank back on the seat, considering. "I guess he wanted to make sure others witnessed the breakup. But why was that important?"

A thought occurred to me as she described their dinner blow-by-blow. "Is it possible he was protecting you?"

She jerked. "You think he knew he was a target for murder and he was trying to shield me?"

Wickersham was smart. All it took was my question and she caught on immediately to the significance of what could've been the reason for Craddock's changed feelings. She blinked several times, but tears still appeared. "If that's true, it means he still cared for me. More than I realized."

"It's just a theory, Harper," I replied. "But if we're right, it could mean he knew something was coming to a head. Think back. What could he have said to you, even in passing, in the days before that suggested he was worried?"

"I hadn't really talked to him since Thanksgiving, and then he was more interested in getting his full share of the bird and mashed potatoes and then the games afterwards. I was busy with work the days leading up to the holiday. In fact, the night before was when I last used the snake. A young woman in my apartment building called me about nine, freaking out because she'd clogged up her kitchen sink with potato peels. I took pity on her and went to the rescue."

"That explains one of the questions we've had since receiving the medical examiner's report," Herc said. "Apparently there were tiny specs of an unidentified biological residue found in his wound. Could those have been potato peels?"

She put a hand to her mouth. "Unclogging her sink was more complicated than usual because she'd stuck stuff down there that never should've gone down the drain. I was exhausted afterwards and just stuck the snake and my other tools in my pickup and forgot about them. That's so embarrassing. So unprofessional. No good plumber puts their snake away until they've cleaned it thoroughly because there's so much gunk and other nasty things that cling to it as the drain is unclogged."

"And you didn't think about it the next day or next several days?" I asked.

She lowered her eyes briefly. "I swear, this has never happened before. But I overslept the next morning, and since I'd volunteered to pick up the turkey dinner, I went directly there after I showered and dressed. That afternoon, after I learned about Jed's cheating on me, that's all I thought about for the rest of the weekend. Since it was a holiday, I didn't have any work going on until Monday morning, when I saw you. There was no need for the snake that day, so I continued to forget about it. Please don't hold that against me in the future."

"Let's put that fact aside for the moment," I said. "Since you claim you didn't use it to kill Craddock, someone else must have borrowed it from you. When could that have happened?"

"My pickup's parked in a locked garage space when I'm not out on a job. The first time it left the garage was Thanksgiving Day. I parked in the supermarket lot for a few minutes while I raced in and got the dinner. Then I was parked in the studio's lot for that afternoon until a little after five. I stayed home the rest of the weekend licking my wounds. I parked in front of the Mehaffy place all day Monday, and then I drove to our dinner Monday night. Jed wanted to meet me at the restaurant rather than pick me up. I know why now. I came directly home that night and didn't go out again until Tuesday morning, when I again was at the project. That's the morning you caught me lighting into my crew member. Monday and Tuesday nights, I stopped at a fast food place for dinner and then parked in the garage as soon as I got home."

"Thanksgiving Day, Sunday night, Monday or Tuesday," Herc said. "How can we narrow it down?"

"I can't swear to it," she said, "but I always keep the pickup locked. Too many valuable tools inside." She snorted. "And yet that's what had to have happened."

"At any of those times, did you notice the locks could've been jimmied?"

She shook her head. "Wait. When I got to the studio on Thanksgiving, my arms were full carrying the meal. It's possible I didn't lock the car behind me in my rush to get inside and unload everything."

"What about when you left that day?" I asked. "Did you notice it was unlocked?"

"No. It could've been. My mind was on Jed sleeping with Lola and on getting away from there as soon as possible."

Herc pivoted more toward her. "It's possible someone at the studio could've borrowed the snake while it was there that day."

"That limits us to Compton, Drysdale and Lola Benson," I said, "since we've been told the Sheldons had taken Helena Sheldon's mother out for lunch."

"No, they were back by four," Wickersham said. "Helena stopped by to check on things. I got the impression she didn't believe the four of them could actually spend the afternoon together without a major confrontation."

"What about Bart Sheldon? Did he return also?" Herc asked.

"I can't say. I assume he was back, too, but I didn't see him," she replied.

I tried not to exchange glances with Herc, but this could be the piece of hard evidence we'd been seeking. I didn't want to get her excited yet. "Anything else you might have noticed about your pickup, the equipment inside or anyone who may have shown too much interest in your vehicle?"

She seemed to realize this was not a subject to be dismissed because she took her time answering. "When I use the snake, like the night before Thanksgiving, I wear a pair of heavy disposable gloves to avoid any part of my body coming in touch with whatever gunk could collect on the coil. I throw them away afterwards, which I did that night after I tossed the snake in my pickup. If whoever stole my snake intended to use it to strangle Jed, would they have thought to use gloves as well?"

"Are you suggesting they didn't use gloves?" Herc asked.

Wickersham wasn't about to drop her theory, having found a

way to remove the onus from herself. "Someone who didn't know a thing about plumbing might not have known it was practice to use them. But on the other hand, if they planned to kill him with it from the start, they probably wore some kind of gloves to keep their fingerprints off the snake. But would they have known to use heavy disposal gloves? What if they wore some other kind of glove, like a work glove? Most likely, they destroyed them afterwards. But, and this is a huge but, what if they didn't? What if they simply hid them somewhere?"

"You're right, that's a huge but," Herc said.

I wasn't as ready to dismiss the idea, as far-fetched as it seemed at the moment. "The medical examiner projects the time of death sometime between six thirty and seven that night, when he was found. That's a very small window. Following through on Harper's last supposition, what if they were in a rush for some reason and didn't have time to get rid of them?"

I shouldn't be saying all this in front of Wickersham, but since she was the one who'd begun this train of thought and knew the most about the use of the weapon, she might as well hear my thoughts. Yes, I was rationalizing, but this had taken on life so quickly, there wasn't time to handle it the proper way.

"You're grasping at straws, Ro," Herc said, momentarily forgetting Wickersham was there.

"Probably, but this gives us probable cause to search the studio."

"Watkins will never sign off on this, let alone a judge," Herc said.

"We have to try. Even if we get the warrant to search the premises and don't find anything, we'll at least have eliminated the possibility of finding the gloves."

"And have run the risk of revealing our biggest clue to date."

"That's all I can remember," Wickersham said, reminding us she was still present. "If anything more comes back to me about the snake, I'll let you know immediately. But for now, it sounds like you've got things to discuss without me in the back seat." She opened the door.

"Before you go, Harper, thanks. Remembering all the details about your breakup has to have been difficult if not also humiliating. Thanks for your help," I said.

"Yeah, thanks," Herc said begrudgingly. "It goes without saying, keep this to yourself."

"I want you to find his killer as much as you do. Maybe more. If he hadn't been killed, maybe Jed and I could've worked things out in the long run," she replied. She shut the door and ran into the house.

Herc watched her go. "I'm not crazy about sharing so much with her."

"She shared even more with us, Herc. She may have helped us crack the case."

"Don't get ahead of yourself. This glove theory is very tenuous. I don't want to put so much faith in it that we miss what could be the real clue."

"Could we at least talk to Jim?"

"Captain Watkins, in this case. I guess so. It's the best thing we've got going at the moment."

CHAPTER 24

"We'll have to convince Jim there's probable cause," I said more to myself than to Herc as we discussed getting a warrant.

"Do you think we have it?"

"I think it's there somewhere in all the information we've collected. The problem is, we still haven't isolated the group of suspects to one or two probables. All five occupants of the studio, plus Ackroyd from Craddock's past and even Harper Wickersham, had motives. I just don't see how we'll get any deeper just from talking to them. We need something more solid. The gloves could do it."

"Normally I'd suggest we get coffee or something to eat while we let our brains recalibrate, but once we've finished eating or drinking, we'll still be at this same point," he said miserably, apparently stuck.

I was just as stuck, but it was my turn to be positive. "Why don't we go over our notes and the medical examiner's report and see if anything jumps out at us that we've missed so far."

We both opened our notebook computers and pulled up our case notes. Neither of us spoke for a few minutes while each of us reviewed the data in our own way. I went directly to the medical examiner's report. It had come in late the day before. We were still absorbing its contents.

"Let's talk to the medical examiner in person," I said. "I want to go over his report line by line."

Herc didn't object, so we called Whip Kelsey, the ME, and asked to meet with him.

"You caught me at just the right time. I was about to call it a day," Kelsey said once we were seated in his office. "How can I clarify my report? I thought it was pretty specific." He didn't appear to be offended.

"How sure are you that death was caused by strangulation by the plumber's snake?" I asked, taking the lead.

"One hundred percent sure. It could've been easy to assume the snake did it, since it was found so close to the body. But examination of the tool revealed physical evidence from the victim on one spot near the middle, indicating it was the point of contact with the victim's jugular."

"In other words, we're not wasting our time concentrating on the snake?"

"No."

"We want to go back over the part of the report that describes the other matter besides the victim's that was found on the snake," Herc said. "The report says it consisted of various samples of organic material. Were you able to identify it more specifically?"

"I could only take an educated guess, which is why I described it in broader terms in the report. It appeared to be bits of potato peel and apple peel, like someone who didn't know better would attempt to place in their garbage disposal."

"Where was this material found?" I asked.

"All over the snake but particularly near the auger end. I have to say, I was surprised to find so much detritus on this tool. It's my understanding these are cleaned thoroughly after each use to avoid the spread of bacteria. That wasn't the case here."

"Could the killer have strangled the victim using the snake as a garotte with their bare hands?" Herc asked.

Kelsey rubbed a cheek. "It would've been more difficult to get a good grip on it, but I guess it could've been done. Didn't find any discernable fingerprints on it, though."

"Is there any way to tell if the killer used their bare hands or gloves?" I asked.

He tilted his head to the side. "We didn't find any traces of human skin along other sections of the coil than the part that touched the victim's throat. There were some unidentified flecks of some type of material. Just a trace. But they could've been from gloves. Not the vinyl or synthetic disposable type. Heavier cloth gloves."

"Interesting theory," Captain James Watkins said after the two of us finished laying out our thoughts about the gloves. "Suppose such items actually exist and you find them hidden somewhere at the old motel. And analysis shows the same matter we found on Craddock. What have you got then?"

"Proof that someone at the studio did the deed," I said, knowing my response was fraught with holes.

"What kind of proof?" Jim asked.

"Possible fingerprints either inside or outside the gloves," I replied.

"Outside might be possible, if our culprit wasn't cautious and left them there. What about inside?"

"DNA."

He nodded, conceding the point.

"If we find them in someone's room or living quarters, we can assume the gloves belong to them."

"Really? What's to say they weren't hidden in that location to point the finger at someone else? Even Harper Wickersham could've done that. Then she could conveniently suggest the idea to the two of you at a later time in an attempt to throw suspicion elsewhere."

I tried another tact. "Suppose we do find them in someone's room or living quarters? We can put them on the spot and see if they confess." That sounded implausible, even to me.

"What's your take on this, Morgan?" Jim asked Herc, who hadn't said anything since introducing the subject.

"It's worth a shot, especially if the warrant's general enough to include items other than the gloves," Herc replied. "We have five possible suspects who reside at the studio. They all have motives for killing the guy, but so far, everything we've learned from them is hearsay, the most important report being that Craddock was a blackmailer. Even if we don't find the gloves, we may still uncover other evidence leading to the killer."

"I'll trust your assessment, you two. I've seen you pull rabbits out of hats we didn't even know existed. Don't let me down," Jim said. He rose from behind his desk, where he'd been seated throughout our weak attempt to get his approval. He came around and leaned against the front. "Our first shot at a warrant is our best shot. We don't want to spend our authority without being able to back it up."

Was Jim just posturing for the sake of being the grown-up in this meeting, or was he really concerned about our chances of making this stick? "Does that mean you'll approve this action, Captain?" Herc asked.

"What would you two do? You've both been around longer than me."

"With respect, Captain, it's not our decision to make," Herc said.

"Of course, it's not, but how would you answer?" Watkins asked again.

"We wouldn't be here if I didn't think I'd answer yes," I said. "Lieutenant Morgan agreed to accompany me and not protest if you agreed."

"Morgan isn't working for us in a consultant capacity," the Captain said.

In other words, I didn't have as much to lose as Herc. But since he'd placed me in this position, I argued my case. "Exactly, Captain. I'm consulting because you, and therefore the department, respect my years of experience and close rate."

Jim nodded. "You make an excellent point, Ro. I'll call the judge. It's up to her to decide. Be ready to present the same arguments to her."

"Thanks, Jim, uh, Captain," I said, almost running from his office, Herc right behind me.

"Hope you're satisfied," Herc said when we were safely away from Jim's hearing.

"I had a hunch. I had to go with it."

"Good thing I learned to trust your hunches years ago, or I'd be as leery as Watkins."

"The judge still has to agree, and she's a stickler."

With our input, mainly mine, Janet Oliver prepared our request for the warrant.

"What do we do while we wait?" Herc asked once the Captain had signed off on the request.

"Get your people ready. If we get the judge's okay, we'll need a comprehensive team to help us search that large structure simultaneously. Let's go to the conference room and pull up the blueprints Donahue sent us and start formulating a plan of attack. We'll probably get only one chance to do this, so we'd better be prepared to cover as much territory as we can."

"Besides looking for the gloves?" he asked.

"Lola Benson should have the books by now, so we won't need to search for those. But this could be our best shot at finding any evidence that Bart Sheldon has been dealing in stolen goods, not that I have any hopes of finding anything of substance. Sheldon's too smart to bring in anything while we're still hanging around."

"In other words, scour every room for proof of something that won't be there just to prove it's not there?"

"Sounds crazy when you put it like that, but yes. I want to take another look at the murder room."

"The crime scene team went over the floor thoroughly. We did, too."

"Plus Compton snuck in even though he wasn't supposed to. Maybe Drysdale did the same or one of the others? Enough to scatter elsewhere whatever may have been left there," I said. I was probably needlessly building up my hopes, but I thought there was still a possibility we'd missed something.

"Okay. I trust your judgment," Herc said.

"Has your team finished going through Craddock's phone-call history and messages?"

"You should have that report in your file. I scanned it last night and didn't find much."

"That alone should tell us something. He didn't call or text anyone at the studio suggesting he knew something they didn't want him to know. If he was blackmailing anyone there, he must've done it in person."

"Still, it won't hurt to go through his room another time now to see if there's any trace of info he has on someone," Herc said.

"Legally, the suspects have every right to be on the premises while the search is conducted, but if they don't object, let's detain them in one of those larger rooms on the first floor while we're there."

"If they don't object?" Herc snorted. "We can try, but I wouldn't characterize the five of them as cooperative. I predict they'll be having fits as soon as they learn about the search."

He studied me, like there was more he wanted to say. "It's not like you to let details like lurking suspects bother you. Why this time?"

I had to think about his question before answering. "You're right. I think it's because they're all there in one place. Not that we haven't encountered similar situations in the past. But ever since our first arrival on the scene, I've had this feeling they were ready for us, that any shred of evidence had already been removed."

"What's so different about that? It happens more often than we want to admit."

"It's not like we haven't encountered suspects who we find as irritating as the five at the studio. There've been plenty in the past. I just get this feeling that none of them are working in concert. They're each out for their own good. Yet their actions, though independent, seem orchestrated for the sole purpose of subverting our investigation. How is that the case? The only one who might care about one of the others is Helena and her feelings for Bart. She may claim to love her daughter, but the fact that she's almost completely emptied the trust fund says otherwise. Whatever Lola felt for her is gone now that she's learned about the trust fund."

Herc rubbed his head. "All that touchy-feely stuff makes my head spin. I don't have any answers for you, Ro, because those thoughts hadn't occurred to me. I'm just 'see the world as it is Morgan.' But since you seem to need some kind of reassurance from me, here's my advice: we put them in a room with one of our officers guarding them and then we forget all about them until we need to search that room. Out of sight, out of mind."

I gave his suggestion some thought. Since I couldn't come up with anything better on my own, it sounded like a plan.

CHAPTER 25

The judge signed the warrant the next morning. Herc and his team moved in immediately, and I went with them. Bart Sheldon tried to leave the premises but was caught by two officers and brought to what they called their training room. Protesting the entire time that the police had no right to invade his private property, he was immediately on his phone supposedly consulting an attorney, all the time demanding to see the warrant.

Helena Sheldon was still getting dressed when she was served. She, too, complained we had no right to be there. She was allowed to finish dressing while a female officer stayed with her.

Lola Benson was still asleep and had to be roused. Another female officer stayed with her while she dressed. I was told later that Benson's only reaction was that the books she'd made her mother turn over to her not be removed from her quarters as they were now part of a suit against her mother and grandmother.

Compton was in the pool doing early morning laps. He threw on his swim robe and grabbed his phone before accompanying the officer assigned to him to the training room.

Drysdale was just returning to the building with a fast food bag containing his breakfast. He was allowed to finish it in the lobby so he wouldn't have to fight off the others, who probably hadn't eaten yet.

Though the police department didn't make it a practice to feed people displaced by searches, we provided doughnuts and coffee to the group in the training room, since we'd showed up so early and they'd be cloistered for a couple of hours. Fed, they might be less argumentative. Once all five arrived, one officer remained posted there while the others headed off to their assigned locations.

We started with the fitness room. "I know you think I'm crazy for coming back here when it's been swept by our techs, but I just want to assure myself we didn't miss anything," I told Herc as we entered.

"Your hunches have worked well in the past. If one more time through helps reassure you this room is clean of any additional evidence, I'm game to try."

At the entrance, we both put on booties, since we didn't want to contaminate anything that might still be on the floor.

At first glance, the area around the stationary bike showed nothing. The same for our second pass.

"Satisfied?" Herc asked.

"Does this thing move?" There didn't appear to be anything attaching the stationary bike to the floor, but my efforts to push it to the side weren't working.

"Here, let me help," Herc said, taking hold of the bar that ran from the seat to the front console. Together, we were able to slide the bike a tad to the left. When we checked the floor we'd uncovered, we found a few specs of something. Couldn't make out the color for sure. It could've been white, cream, or even a pale yellow.

"I think we've found a few tiny particles from a glove, Herc," I said, not believing we'd actually found something.

"Don't get excited yet," he said, using a pair of tweezers to bag the residue.

"It's possible those got blown there by someone's foot pushing them out of the way, like

when Compton and Drysdale were attempting to get the body off the bike."

Herc rolled his eyes but didn't dispute me any further.

Although we checked out the rest of the room, we didn't find anything else of note, so we moved on to the living quarters.

We went next to the Sheldons' apartment. My first observation was that they'd never win an award for their housekeeping skills. Their sloppiness made our search more difficult because we had to lift clothes, papers and other garbage with tongs rather than flip through neat piles. Our next discovery was that the Sheldons appeared to be sleeping in different beds. Helena Sheldon's room had a private entrance. Probably how she slipped Compton in and out for their private get-togethers.

Her wardrobe filled two closets, one lounging chair and half the floor. How much of Lola's trust fund purchased these items? The woman probably called them business expenses.

We found a safe in the larger closet. Locked, of course. Although the warrant covered such a contingency, we couldn't open it without getting the code from her or with the help of a locksmith. Choosing the first option, we called Ennis and had him escort Helena back to her apartment.

"Absolutely not!" Her voice reached new levels. "It's bad enough you've been treating us like criminals, locking us up in our own studio. You have no right to open my safe."

"Actually, the warrant we served you says we do," Herc told her in his official voice. "We're required to ask you to either open it or give us the code first, but if you refuse and we believe there could be something inside pertinent to our investigation, we'll call in a locksmith, who might be able to determine the code but more likely will have to cut it open."

She took a step back, her lips pulled in. "All right, all right. The sooner you get off our backs, the better. But that doesn't mean I'll let you take possession of whatever might be in there."

"That depends on what we find. If it's evidence, we may have to impound it."

"I want to call my lawyer first."

"Fine," Herc replied. "Do it now."

Her attorney wanted Herc to read the relevant parts of the warrant to him over the phone before advising Helena. Once he got the gist of our search, he told Helena she would have to comply, but she also had the right to be there while the safe was opened and the contents examined.

We pulled in another officer to join the one with Helena so they could witness and film what we removed from the inside, which turned out to be over a hundred and fifty thousand dollars in cash. More of the trust fund? We asked, but her attorney had told her she didn't have to reply, so she clammed up. If I had seen any maternal instincts in Helena Sheldon before, this totally nailed shut that door, although she'd probably claim she was keeping the money safe for Lola.

"I want a copy of that videotape when you leave," she said as she left with her guard. "And I expect to find every dollar of that money still in the safe when I'm allowed to return."

We didn't answer. The less said to the woman right now the better.

Our search uncovered a pair of gardening gloves found in one of the drawers in her kitchen cabinet and a pair of heavy rubber gloves located under the kitchen sink. We also found a gun in the nightstand drawer next to her bed.

Bart Sheldon's room wasn't much tidier than his wife's. At least they had that much in common. Judging from the fast food trash strewn about the place, he apparently had a lot of his meals in here. A collection of girlie magazines was found under the mattress. He hadn't evolved to porn he could stream on television.

Herc found three guns of varying caliber in the closet. One was loaded, like Bart was expecting trouble at any minute.

Not surprisingly, we found no compromising materials

concerning whatever extracurricular activities he was involved in. Would've been nice. More than nice. But the man was no fool when it came to questionable activities.

We did find a pair of gloves, though. Heavy industrial-strength work gloves tucked away in a sock drawer. Used, too, by the creases and debris on the palms. We stuck them in two separate evidence bags like we had with each of Helena's gloves. These would be sent to Dr. Kelsey for examination as soon as possible.

Herc shot a backward glance at the Sheldons' apartment as we left. "Don't like leaving those guns behind, but we had no call to take them."

"At this point," I said.

"For future reference, though, remember what he's got in his arsenal. And that was just his bedroom."

We went through Lola Benson's suite of rooms next. I went right to the set of books on her kitchen counter. When Lola had demanded them from her mother, I assumed she meant computer files, but apparently Helena Sheldon preferred paper accounts. Or perhaps she didn't know how to keep them online.

I quickly flipped through them, like I was some kind of accounting savant. It would take longer than a few seconds to absorb the overall condition, but the lengthy list of red numbers on the expenses page screamed financial trouble.

We pretty much knew that. And so did Lola, who was already on it.

Herc scoured the kitchen. "How long is dressing supposed to last?" he asked from inside the fridge.

"Two to three days. Why?"

"Ms. Benson seems to be raising her own petri dish. Suppose she doesn't know these things have expiration dates?"

"She probably goes into her fridge once a day for milk for her cereal and doesn't pay much attention to anything else."

Though not all her clothes had been put away, she at least was into folding and stacking them. Her mother would be so proud.

The bed was unmade, but then, she'd still been asleep when we arrived.

Although we didn't find any type of glove, we did find a packet of a white powdery substance. She hadn't come across as a druggie, but some people were very good at hiding highs. I showed Herc what I'd found. "Cocaine?" I asked.

He shrugged. "Beats me. I never got very good at identifying stuff like that. We'll have to wait until Kelsey does his thing with it."

"Do you think it could be poison?" I asked.

"In a separate packet like that? I suppose, but that would mean she was intending it for something other than getting high. Like maybe to use on someone?"

He took the packet from me, carefully smelled the contents, then handed it back. "Don't know what I thought I'd be able to detect. Kelsey's gonna be busy for a while."

"If it's poison, Lola just moved up the suspect list."

"If it is, who was it intended for?" Herc asked.

"Most likely her mother, although possibly she'd add Bart to the list, depending on whether she thinks he talked Helena into scamming her."

"Not Craddock?" Herc asked.

"Until we learned she'd been selling stolen cell phones on campus, I had her pegged as a ditsy innocent, but that piece of information changed how I view her."

"But she wasn't smart enough to discover what her mother was doing to her trust fund."

Good point. "True."

"And what motive would she have had for killing Craddock?"

"Another good point," I said. "Unless we've missed something? Perhaps there was more to their brief fling than we know."

"Let's not get caught up speculating about Lola Benson now. We've got to be alert while we check the other rooms."

"Who's next?" I asked.

"Compton, I guess."

Compton had cleaned up his room since we were last here. With the exception of a stack of folded towels, everything was neat and orderly. No gloves, although we did find a ball bat we confiscated and several cans and jars of bodybuilding supplements. "Since when does a male model need to build up his body?" I asked Herc.

He pulled the lid off one and checked the contents, sniffing first, then tasting a few particles that stuck to his index finger. "This stuff smells okay, but we might as well take it to Kelsey for testing. For all we know, someone may have salted this stuff with poison or drugs."

"What do you think the ball bat is for?" I asked.

"Baseball?"

"I know that, but did you find a glove or balls with it?"

"Uh, no, but that's not necessarily suspicious," Herc said. "He may have bought it for pickup games."

"Or he got it to defend himself against any further attacks," I said. Was I reading too much into this? But I had to at this point, until we were ready to zero in on the real killer.

As it turned out, Drysdale was a minimalist. Funny we hadn't noticed that tendency when we interviewed him before, but our minds were on him then, not his surroundings. His wardrobe was sparse. Everything was either hung up or stored away in his bureau drawers. And yet I got the feeling that this was all a stage set laid out to convince us or anyone else who visited this room that nothing was going on.

"We need to search this one well, Herc, especially hidden places."

We spent the next fifteen minutes running our hands carefully along walls, baseboards, inside drawers, whatever appeared to be perfectly ordinary. Every so often we'd get lucky. The first time we found a hundred dollars, probably stuck away to remove it from temptation. Inside the top of a drawer, his passport. Taped behind the bureau, a list of what appeared to be computer passwords.

His refrigerator contained very little except for a few bottles of some kind of liquid. Two were orange, the third clear. Herc held it up for a closer look. "Ever seen a bottle like this?"

I took hold of it and brought it closer to my eyes. "No, I haven't. It could be spring water, but I've always seen that in plastic bottles, not those made of glass."

Herc bagged it too. "I'll probably be proven wrong, but since everyone else seems to have found their weapon of choice, I'm not dismissing this liquid."

It wasn't until we checked the gym bag set far back in Drysdale's closet that we found another pair of industrial gloves. Traces of a gray-brown substance had dried on the palms.

"That leaves only Craddock's room to go over again," Herc said.

My phone rang as we approached his door. It was Harper Wickersham. "You said to call if I thought of anything else about that last dinner with Jed. He said something weird to me just as I was leaving, but I've been so wrapped up in his dumping me and then his murder, I hadn't thought about it until just now."

"What did he say?" I tried not to sound too impatient, but I wanted to get on with this search.

"As I was getting ready to leave, I dropped my car keys. For some reason that's still unclear to me, he didn't reach down to retrieve them. He let me do that. 'If anything should happen to me, know that you've been the one ray of sunshine in my life these past months,' he said. Everyone seated around us had heard him tell me we were done. All I wanted to do was get out of there with as much dignity as possible. It wasn't until now that I've started to wonder why he said that if he no longer wanted to be with me."

"You're right. That does sound strange. We're sort of busy with another aspect of the case at the moment. How 'bout I get back to you later? Maybe we can consider his intention together."

"I'll be at the Mehaffy site if you need me."

Her timing was ironic, since we were just about to go back in Craddock's room.

I forgot her call as we opened the door.

"What the …?" Herc said.

The room had been turned upside down since we'd last been here, despite the crime scene tape across the door. The mattress and bedding had been pulled off the bed. All the clothes that had once hung in the closet or been tucked away in the chest of drawers had been thrown on the floor. Cereal and snack boxes had been ripped open, the contents resting in stacks that looked like anthills.

"So much for crime scene tape," I said, hesitant to step inside.

"Someone was looking for something. Any idea if they found it?" Herc asked.

"Hard to tell. They were definitely in a hurry and didn't care if we discovered their handiwork after the fact."

"Think it's connected to the murder or was someone just helping themselves to Craddock's things?"

"I doubt they would have pursued this type of selection process if they were after something of his," I said. "But since they didn't take time to conduct a tidy search, I'd say they were desperate. They may even have anticipated our search today and had to get whatever it was out of here before we found it."

"Should we assume they found it?" Herc asked.

I shook my head in frustration. "I don't know. They may have been unsuccessful, and this little display was simply to slow us down."

"In other words, we still have to do our thing in here. We can assume all the more obvious places have already been covered, so we focus on potential hiding places."

For the next twenty minutes we tapped walls, examined baseboards and felt our way through empty drawers to no avail.

Finally, Herc was ready to hoist the white flag. "We haven't found anything of note here. I say we move on."

"Before we do, let's take a minute to analyze where this leaves us. Craddock apparently had something someone else wanted. More than likely, it wasn't money. He didn't appear to have much.

I doubt he had any jewelry or treasure maps. And his computer and TV set are still here, untouched. That brings us back to what we heard from Drysdale: Craddock was blackmailing someone. They shortsightedly killed the guy before they got what he had on them. This mess tells us that."

"What do you propose we do about it?"

"I'm not sure, Herc. I think the best we've got so far are a few pairs of gloves to check for residue plus cash in Helena Sheldon's safe, various weapons and possible poisonous substances. I don't know that we'll find anything more of interest here, so let's have the rest of the crew finish the search while we turn in what we've found thus far to Kelsey."

CHAPTER 26

We dropped off our evidence with Dr. Kelsey, who we'd put on alert so he could get right to it.

While we waited for the results, I remembered the phone call I'd received from Harper Wickersham just as we were about to enter Craddock's room. I'd spaced off on it as soon as I saw how the room had been trashed. "Let's go talk to Wickersham at Mehaffy House. I cut her off on her phone call. After discovering Craddock's room had been invaded, I'm beginning to think maybe there was something more to what he told her that night at the restaurant."

We found Val working on the front stairs when we arrived. "Didn't expect to see you here today, Mom," she said.

"Actually, we're here to see Harper Wickersham. Why are you working on the stairs? They're not scheduled until later in the project."

"Just doing a structural check today. But I noticed there's a piece missing from the newel post. Harper's out in the kitchen checking the pipes."

"That's right. The top piece, the finial, needed some attention, so I must've stuck it in my bag and forgotten about it. I'll look for it when I get home."

We left Val and wandered out to the kitchen.

"Sorry I had to cut you off earlier," I told her when she glanced up from the pipes she was examining.

"I figured something big was about to go down. Does that mean you arrested Jed's killer?"

"Sorry, not yet," Herc replied. "We're here because we want to follow up on your last time with Craddock."

"Let me get out of this cramped position. We can talk on the front porch." Once we were all seated on the steps, she began. "That last evening is all I've been able to think about this morning." She realized that might not have been the smartest thing to say in front of her employer. "Of course, I've still been concentrating a hundred percent on this job. But apart from that, the scene from that night kept looping through my mind."

"Any new insights?" I asked.

"It was so unlike Jed. Not just his breaking up with me but the way he told me. We rarely had dinner dates, especially at a nice family place like The Sandpiper. He chose that setting. At first I thought we went there because someone had told him to break up in a public place so the other person couldn't go ballistic on him. But he also used what sounded like a stage voice so others could hear. I've been asking myself why he did that. I'd thought at first it was to embarrass me, but I now wonder if it wasn't to go on record that I was no longer part of his life. Like to protect me, you know?"

"That's an interesting theory," I replied. "Protect you from what or whom?"

"I haven't figured out that part yet. He didn't warn me, at least not in so many words, although he did say, 'If something should happen to me.' That was pretty dramatic, now that I look back on it, but at the time, I just wanted to get out of there. That's probably why I dropped my keys, although that was fishy also. Just as I was retrieving them, his hand shot out, knocking them out of my hands. I dismissed it as an accident, but that could've been done on purpose. He didn't apologize or even bother to stoop over and get them for me."

While she described that dinner, I'd attempted to picture it in my head. She was right. His actions were strange, but they were telling us something. "How long did you lean over to get the keys?" I asked.

"Just seconds, although longer than you'd think because they didn't fall directly under the table. They were about a foot away. Far enough that I had to get off my chair and stoop way down."

"Show us," I said.

She didn't argue. I handed her my keys, and she stepped down to the landing and went through the motions. I counted off twelve seconds in my head.

"What were you wearing, Harper?"

"My best jeans and a lightweight pullover."

"No jacket or coat?"

"No."

"How about a purse?"

She considered. "Yes. By then, it was setting right on the table as I prepared to leave. I'd opened it to get my keys." My question triggered a thought. "You think he used that time to put something in my purse?"

"It's possible," I replied cautiously, trying to keep my own mounting excitement under control as much as hers. "Given how you've described his actions and words being so unlike him."

Herc cut us off. "Where is your purse?"

"Locked in my pickup. Should I get it?"

"I'll get it," Herc said. "Just give me the keys."

Her face took on a confused expression, but she did as he directed. She might not have realized that he wasn't taking any chances of her taking off on us with what could be a huge breakthrough in the case.

He returned a minute later, purse in hand, and offered it to her. "Should I dump all the contents on the porch floor?" she asked.

I handed her a pair of disposable gloves. "Let's take it slower and examine the contents piece by piece."

The first item removed was a change purse. She opened it and emptied two dimes, a nickel and a penny into the palm of her left hand. "These don't appear to be anything but real coins." She set them on the porch. Next came a wallet containing several bills and her credit cards. She handed them to Herc to examine. She didn't carry much cash, maybe nineteen dollars. She must depend on her credit cards.

Herc shook his head after giving each bill and card a thorough once-over.

She continued to remove the contents: two tubes of lipstick, one tube of lip balm, a few tissues and a sunglasses case.

"That's all there is," she said.

"What did you say he told you right after he said something about if you should never see him again?" I asked.

She thought a bit. "Know that you've been the one ray of sunshine in my life these past months." She brightened. "The sunglasses case!"

The case was one of those squeeze-tops where a pair of folded glasses could just be stuck in. Wickersham removed the glasses. Enmeshed in the arms was a flash drive. She carefully removed it and handed it to me. "This isn't mine. I've never seen it before."

Herc wore a skeptical expression. "He had all of twelve seconds to get it in there. That's not a lot of time."

"It's more than possible. Remember what I told you about Jed being an amateur magician? He used to show me some of his sleight-of-hand tricks."

I took a couple of deep breaths, willing myself to stay in professional mode and not get too carried away with this discovery until we checked it out. "It would appear he wanted you to have this in case anything happened to him. We won't know for sure until we view the contents."

"I want to see it too." Her voice carried a steely resolve.

"I'm sorry, Harper," I said. "This is now in police custody."

"Look, I've cooperated a hundred percent with you guys. I may have just helped you solve this case. I want to be there to see what it is. He meant it for me."

"Letting you view it at this point would be highly unprofessional," Herc told her.

"I want to be there."

"I see how this looks to you. Like you've just found a pot of gold at the end of the rainbow. But for all we know, you set this up. Everything we know about this flash drive at this point has come from you."

"I didn't set you up! I didn't have to tell you any of this. I could've struggled with this memory and eventually thought about my sunglasses case. Or more likely, it would've fallen out the next time I used them and I would've figured out its significance. And you never would've known."

"But that didn't happen," I said. "We have to take it from there. If this has any bearing on the case, we have to ensure the proper chain of custody."

"What does that mean? That I can never see it?" Her volume had increased to the point where she was shaking.

Herc stepped in with all the authority of the department. "We can't promise you anything until we know more about this."

She quickly dumped everything she'd removed back into her purse. "Do what you have to do. I'm coming to the station with you, and I'm camping out there until you let me see what's on this flash drive."

I gazed at Herc. He sensed I was about to cave. Maybe it wasn't legal or appropriate police procedure, but she deserved to see what she'd turned over to us. Herc closed his eyes once. My cue.

"All right. But only under our conditions. Is that understood?"

She nodded. "I'll wrap up here and meet you at the station."

"She'd better not do anything to jeopardize whatever is on that flash drive," Herc said through gritted teeth as he drove. "She could've been playing us from the very beginning when she demanded you sit in when we first interrogated her. But you've believed her innocent from the start. I hope this isn't the one time your feelings deceive you."

I hoped so, too.

Back at the station, Herc and I went through the proper procedures to ensure there would be no future question about our maintaining the chain of custody. Janet Oliver played the flash drive. Wickersham was allowed to sit nearby and told not to talk until the flash drive had completely played.

Everything was dark at first. Probably shot at night. Gradually, our eyes adjusted to the dim view. Three male figures came into view, Bart Sheldon and two unidentified men, and we realized we were gazing down on the scene. From the walkway on the second floor? All three men were carrying boxes out of one of the rooms on the first floor and taking them around the building to the back, presumably to a waiting vehicle.

One of the men set down his box and opened it with a box cutter. He pulled out a small rectangular box. Then the audio kicked in. "These look like primo cell phones, Sheldon. Where'd they come from?"

"Shh! Keep your voices down. Never can tell who might be up and about in this place," Sheldon said in a lowered voice.

"At three in the morning?" the second guy said, still not lowering his voice.

Sheldon checked back over his shoulder a couple of times. "Just hurry up and get these loaded. I don't want them on my hands any longer. One of the guys here has been acting mighty suspicious."

"I know someone who can shut him up," the first guy said.

"Forget it. I'll handle him, if it comes to that. Just get this load delivered."

"When do we get paid?" the second said.

"When you get these delivered without any fuss. Got it? Don't draw any attention to yourselves. And don't think you can help yourselves to any of the goods. I got in serious trouble a while back when my brat of a stepdaughter thought she could help herself to a small stash."

"Yeah, what happened?"

"You don't want to know. Just keep your hands clean."

The men didn't say much after that as they focused on moving the boxes out of the building, but the video and audio continued.

They were just finishing when Sheldon held up a hand. "Who's there?"

No response.

"Didn't you hear that?" Sheldon whispered to the two men.

"Uh, no," the first guy replied. "You're imagining things, Sheldon."

Sheldon continued to eye the area around him, going as far as the door to the pool area to check there.

"You need to chill, man. Another five minutes and these phones will be nothing but a pleasant memory. You'll have your cut soon."

That said, the two men slipped around the side of the building for the last time. Sheldon moved out of the shot. And the video ended.

I turned to Wickersham. "Any comment?"

She appeared to be stunned as she sat there staring at her clasped hands and shaking her head. "Even if Jed didn't shoot that video, he knew about it. And he was afraid for his life."

"That would appear to be the case," Herc said. "Although he didn't tell you. In fact, he didn't warn you, which placed you in danger too."

"No, he wouldn't do that to me," she replied.

"Most likely, he wasn't thinking that far in advance," I said, again playing the scene out in my mind. "If he was fearing for his life, he was concerned Bart Sheldon knew he had the video. In the scene we viewed, Sheldon thought someone was watching. Somehow he learned it was Craddock." I was ninety-five percent convinced Craddock had tried to blackmail the man and his plan had backfired, but I wasn't ready to run that scenario past Wicker-sham. Yet.

"Am I in danger?" she asked.

"I wouldn't take chances if I were you," I told her. "Do you have somewhere else to stay at night?"

"I have a girlfriend, but I don't want to put her in danger too. Plus, I still have work to do at Mehaffy House."

"I'll see what kind of protective custody I can arrange," Herc said. "We're getting close to making our case, but we're not there yet."

"Even with this video?" she asked.

"It could be enough to arrest him for dealing in stolen goods," Herc said, "although the actual goods are gone. But it's not enough to tie him to the killing."

"Then get busy and do it." She was screaming now as panic overtook her.

Herc excused himself for several minutes. He returned with a female officer. "This is Officer Carol Stone. She'll go with you to your apartment to pack a bag, and then the two of you will head off to a safe house. Mrs. Summerfield here will have to figure out how to deal with the plumbing situation on her project."

To my surprise and relief, Wickersham went willingly.

"Now then," Herc said, once she was gone, "let's find out what Kelsey discovered."

CHAPTER 27

"I don't know how you did it, and I don't need to know, but you managed to not only find particles from the glove used to choke the victim with the plumber's snake, you found the actual gloves," Kelsey told us as soon as we arrived.

"One hundred percent connection?" Herc asked.

"Yes."

"And?" I pushed. "Who do they belong to?"

"Bart Sheldon."

Can't say I was surprised. But it was good to know our suspicions about the guy had been confirmed.

"That's all we needed," Herc said, turning to leave.

"You know as well as I, Herc, any defense attorney worth their salt can claim the gloves weren't necessarily used by Sheldon," I said once we were on our way to the studio. "They were just found in his private quarters."

"I'm well aware of that, Ro. What we've got to do now is convince him we've got all the pieces that prove he murdered Jed Craddock and get him to confess."

While he drove, I connected him with the rest of the team that was still searching the house. Per Ennis, they were wrapping up the search and had just released the suspects. Not the best news.

"None of the five leave the property," Herc said. He then ordered the team to guard the place until we arrived.

We had to find Bart Sheldon as soon as possible, if he hadn't evaded our team already. We split up once we arrived. Herc and one officer went to the pool area. Another officer and I were on our way to the Sheldon apartment when I heard Herc's voice. "Not so fast, Sheldon. You're under arrest for the murder of Jed Craddock." So much for convincing him to confess.

"Sorry, man. But unless you want to shoot me in the back, I'm outta here."

From where I stood inside the building, I could see Herc and the officer staring down Sheldon, who pointed a gun at them. We had him surrounded, but he was a desperate man. Desperate men did desperate things.

Herc had his gun with him and so did the officer, but neither had drawn. Knowing Herc, he would try to talk Sheldon down before either he or the officer went on the offense.

He could possibly pull off a miracle, but the odds were against him. I needed to do something to help my partner and didn't have much time to make it happen.

I raced up the stairs to the second floor and quietly ran along the walkway, hoping Sheldon would be so focused on Herc he couldn't hear me. Bending my knees, I wrapped my arms around the nearest planter. Hoisting it wasn't easy, but I finally managed. I waited for just the right moment.

Herc continued. "While your wife's been scamming her daughter's trust fund to run this place, you've been building your own fortune playing middle man on the stolen goods circuit. Jed Craddock somehow got wind of it, filmed it and wanted his cut. You couldn't let that happen, so you strangled him using his girl-friend's plumber's snake to frame her."

I was prepared for Sheldon to deny everything Herc had said, but apparently he thought he was actually about to get away scot free.

"Such a greedy young man. Greedy but overly confident. It

was child's play to take him out, just like it is now with you two. You can't get the draw on me. I'm leaving, and you can't stop me."

Herc and the officer were at a standstill. I needed to break the logjam.

Show time. I raised the planter a little higher, balanced it on the railing and let go. All the time, I said a silent prayer that Herc and the officer hadn't moved.

I heard the crash before I could view the results.

"Nice going, partner," Herc called.

I glanced down, fearing I'd knocked the guy's head off. To my extreme relief, the planter had struck him hard enough to send him flying and knock him out. Herc and the officer had not been touched.

A medical team was rushed to the scene, and Sheldon was taken to the hospital under guard.

I rejoined Herc and the officer, who were processing the scene.

"Thanks, partner," Herc said. "Never thought you'd be an avenging angel from above. You may have just saved our lives. You certainly helped us get our man."

"You're welcome."

"Don't do it again."

HARPER WICKERSHAM ONLY HAD TO STAY IN PROTECTIVE CUSTODY one night. She probably could've returned to her own apartment the same day we arrested Bart Sheldon, but Herc and I wanted to be sure the charges against the man took.

She was back at Mehaffy House the next day. I was still wrapping up the case with Herc, but I stopped by to get an update from Val and Ryder. It had been less than a week since the case had begun, but it felt like a lot more time had elapsed.

"Congratulations on wrapping the case," she said when she first saw me. "You said you were close, but until you had that creep in custody, I was afraid to believe he could be caught. I just hope the charges stick."

"They should. He admitted he'd killed Jed Craddock not just to Herc but in front of another officer. And a second officer and I witnessed it as well."

"The first thing I did when I heard he'd been arrested was buy another snake. I might've gotten my old one back from you guys eventually, but I could never use it again. Not after ... well, you know."

"I understand."

"You've understood me all along. I can't thank you enough for believing me and looking beyond me as the prime suspect."

"We never totally dismissed you as a suspect. You realize that, I hope?"

She hung her head. "Yeah. But you had to. I get that." I started to go off in search of Val when Wickersham called me back. "I need to earn a living, so I can't provide my service free on this project, but if you ever stop up your sink, give me a call. I've got a new plumber's snake that can really do the job."

EPILOGUE

arrived home to find a container of beef stroganoff waiting for me along with a bouquet of white daisies. "Congratulations!" Chuck said as he breezed into the room. "I heard on the news that you and Herc got your man."

"Sorry, I should've at least texted you, but Herc and I had to brief Jim and the DA once we'd booked Bart Sheldon, and time got away from us."

He raised both hands. "Not to worry. I'm getting accustomed to this routine. You and Morgan have a pretty good track record going. I just hope this means you can take a break from police business for a bit. Christmas is coming, and I'm looking forward to spending the holidays with you."

I went to him and exchanged a long, passionate kiss. The stroganoff and flowers were pretty nice, but this was even better. I was so glad to find him here waiting for me to help me celebrate.

Several minutes and a lot more *us* time later, I pulled away to look for our host. "No Jason yet?"

"Considering his preference for late appearances lately, I wasn't expecting him until you got home. Give him some more time. He'll show up. And in the meantime, let's have some of the dinner Shane Bolton sent home for you. The flowers were my idea."

I had to chuckle. "I think Shane has started getting more into my homicide cases than I ever would've realized."

"Actually, I think he may have an ulterior motive besides wanting to congratulate you."

"Ulterior motive? Did he finally buy some real estate and wants me to renovate it?"

"Uh, no. I shouldn't steal his thunder, but I think he wants to ask you to participate in some event he's part of."

"Event? Like a cooking contest? Or a Christmas party?"

"Ever heard of the Reindeer Run?" Chuck asked, barely able to conceal a smile.

"Reindeer Run? Is that something at the zoo?"

"No, it's a … marathon. A race-type thing, you know?"

"I don't run races."

"Just wait for his call. Don't tell him I said anything."

"Okay. Did he ask you also?"

He made a gesture like he was locking his lips.

"Fine. Keep your secrets. I've got enough on my mind at the moment anyhow. But tonight is reserved for coming down from this case. Got any ideas how I can do that?"

He offered what could only be described as a lascivious look. "I think I can come up with something."

Jason slipped into the room just as we were leaving for the bedroom. "You're late, buddy. You missed your chance to congratulate me as only you can. You'll have to postpone it to morning. Your dinner is waiting for you along with two treats. See ya."

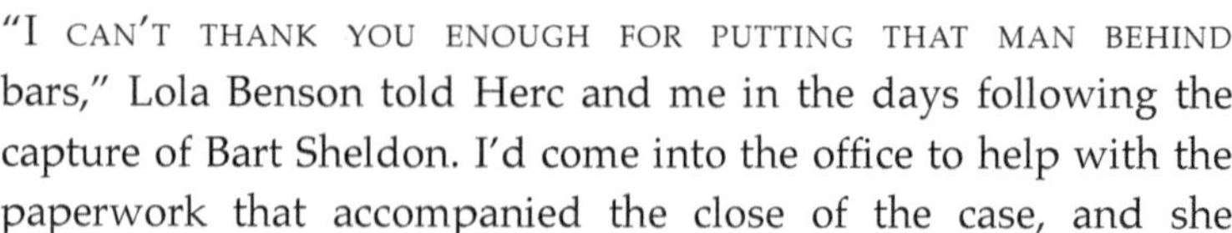

"I can't thank you enough for putting that man behind bars," Lola Benson told Herc and me in the days following the capture of Bart Sheldon. I'd come into the office to help with the paperwork that accompanied the close of the case, and she stopped by to update us about the impact of Sheldon's arrest on the home front. "I'm glad you used my tip about the stolen cell phones. But I had no idea his ties to the underworld went so deep."

"That was a side benefit of getting him for murdering Craddock," Herc said.

"My mother is still reeling. She claims she had no idea he was so involved with stolen goods or that he was capable of killing another person. She's still saying she only had my best interests at heart by using so much of my trust fund. In other words, she's living in her own dream world."

"Are you still suing her to get the rest of the money back?" I asked.

"Yes. I don't like the idea of taking my own mother and grandmother to court, but my attorney told me it's the cleanest way to recoup what I can. The paperwork to change the ownership of the property to me is already underway. I'm letting her continue to live there, but we're switching apartments. I expect her to pay me back some of what she embezzled from me. Possibly by working for me. She isn't really known for her work ethic, so who knows how things will pan out there. Maybe without Bart around to influence her, she'll change."

I doubted that would ever happen, but I wished Lola Benson well.

"What about the business? Will you keep the modeling agency?" Herc asked.

"Joel, Trey and I are discussing our future direction. Joel has indicated an interest in managing the client contacts. He'll do well at that task, once he cuts back on the amount of lemongrass fragrance he's convinced is his trademark. He wasn't crazy about that condition, but I stood firm. The two of us will showcase Trey as our primary talent. Hopefully that will eliminate the competition between the two guys. I plan to run the financial part of the business. Now that I've become somewhat familiar with the books, I feel that's something I could do."

"We wish you luck," I said, really meaning it. "That's a lot of property to manage."

"I agree. We're talking about renting out some of the rooms to college students to bring in additional revenue, but that brings on more liability, which we're not sure we're ready for yet. But thanks to you, the three of us have a future."

I WAS A LITTLE LATE GETTING TO MEHAFFY HOUSE ON MY FIRST FULL day back on the site because I stopped off for doughnuts and coffee for whatever crew was there. I arrived to find Val, Ryder, Wickersham and one of the guys from the electrical crew watching something on Val's laptop. "What's all this? You knew I was bringing goodies?"

"We have something to show you, Mom," Val replied. "Thanks to our electrical genius Dirk here, we've had a bit of a break-through identifying our so-called 'ghosts.' We installed cameras above the side door and on the first floor the last few days, and lo and behold, last night we had visitors."

"Someone was still able to break in, even after we changed all the locks?" I said, confused.

Ryder answered this one. "Turns out there's another entrance in the back of a first-floor closet. Previous owners covered it up on the outside with strategically placed shrubs and an ivy trellis, but it can still be accessed from the outside, if you know how to do it."

I examined the screen more closely. An older man and woman snuck in and cased the place for a few minutes, apparently seeking something to mess with. "Hold on, that's the woman next door and the guy who lives on the other side of this house."

"The neighbors?" Val asked.

"Herc and I attempted to make nice with them last week when we asked if they'd noticed anyone or anything strange going on here. They failed to mention that was them."

"Any idea why they want us to believe the house is haunted?" Ryder asked.

The house wasn't haunted. I'd known that, hadn't I? All along I'd refused to believe we were dealing with ghosts or the paranormal. Okay, there might have been a few moments when I wondered if something beyond my comprehension was going on in this house. But only a few. Ryder's question brought me back to the real world. "Offhand, I'd say they don't want us to renovate the house and sell to new neighbors. I don't know why unless they've grown accustomed to what they think is their privacy."

"What do you want to do about it?" Val asked.

"What do you want to do, partner?" I replied.

"My first inclination is to board up the entrance inside the closet and let them get surprised the next time they decide to create a little havoc."

"What's your second inclination?" I asked her.

She made a face. "I hate it when you make me act like an adult. I suppose we need to confront them. At least find out why they're so opposed to our renovations and see if there isn't some way we can appease them without compromising our own goals."

"Now that we've solved that puzzle, I'll let the two of you figure out what to do about those folks. I need to check on one of my other projects," Ryder said.

"And I need to get back to my wiring," Dirk said.

In the end, we decided to follow the old adage of attracting more bees with honey than vinegar. Val went over to Alicia Hartwig's place to invite her over, and I got the fun job of inviting the guy on the other side. Never did get his name. Maybe that had been a mistake.

We improvised a small seating arrangement with a few boxes and sawhorses and offered what was left of the doughnuts and coffee. Both refused at first but gave in after a second offer.

"What's this all about?" Alicia Hartwig asked. "From the looks of things, it's too soon for an open house."

"That will hopefully come someday soon," I said. "But first we need to know why the two of you are sneaking into this house at night and doing just enough damage to make us wonder if renovating this property was a good idea."

"Sneaking in?" Her voice rose in indignation. "That's a terrible accusation."

"We have your latest caper on video, Mrs. Hartwig. You're in it too, Mr.—uh—"

"Zumkeller. Wally. How'd you manage that?"

"When weird things started happening after hours, we put in some surveillance cameras," Val said.

Zumkeller glared at Hartwig. "I told ya it was a fool idea, Alicia."

"Fool idea or not," I said, "we want to know why. Surely once we've rehabbed this place, your property values will increase."

Once again, they looked at each other.

"What?" Val asked. "The two of you obviously have talked about what's about to happen. Why not share those thoughts with us?"

"Don't you get it?" Hartwig said. "While this place has sat here vacant all these years, it's been the neighborhood eyesore. Our places didn't look so bad."

"Which worked just fine with us," Zumkeller said. "We both live alone on fixed incomes. We can't afford to compete with what this place is becoming."

I set down my coffee container, dumbfounded. I should've seen this coming, but I'd been so involved with the Craddock case, I'd lost focus. No, I was kidding myself. I'd just been blind to the needs of our two neighbors.

"Wow. In all honesty, we had no idea you might feel like that. And that's our fault. We should've been more sensitive to your feelings. What can we do to help?"

"You gonna remodel our houses free of charge?" Zumkeller asked.

"That wasn't called for, Wally," Hartwig said.

"Probably not, but it's how I feel."

I eyed Val, hoping we were on the same wavelength. "What if my daughter and I were to help you do some fixing up? We can't offer a full-fledged rehab, because we're still trying to establish our business and have to keep our costs down, but perhaps a new coat of paint on your exteriors might help?"

I heard a sound similar to air escaping a bicycle tire coming from my daughter, but she didn't openly object. In fact, she added her own spin. "It might be possible to secure a low-interest loan from one of the banks in town, or there might even be some funding for senior citizens needing a little financial assistance. I'd be happy to look into that for you."

"You tryin' to buy us off?" Zumkeller asked.

I laughed. "A little. Is it working?"

"Maybe not on him," Hartwig said, "but I'm interested."

"We're not promising anything right now," I added. "But what we've proposed isn't just to get your cooperation with our project. We just need to discuss this further before we can tell you anything definitive. Is that enough of a promise for you to forget about your nighttime raids?"

The two seemed to communicate between them that they'd agree to a détente.

Once they left, I drank more coffee and finished a doughnut, processing what had just happened.

"Are you okay, Mom? That was some pretty fast thinking."

"You're okay with it, too, I hope?"

"I just wish we'd figured out their reluctance on our own. I feel a little cheap for having missed it."

"That's what's been going through my head. I think this was a wake-up call for the future of Nailed It Home Renos. We have to be more cognizant of the needs of the community."

"I agree. I don't know how. But this is a start."

I hung around the project a little longer than I needed to, just to get my bearings again. I was about to head back to the office and potential new projects when Val approached me.

"With all the hubbub this morning and solving the case, you probably forgot about that missing piece from the newel post."

"The finial. Right. I did. I'll go back to the duplex now to locate it."

The next morning, I stood alongside Val watching Ryder attach the finial to the newel post. Once it was on, he gave it a pat for good measure. "Ouch!" he cried, withdrawing his hand immediately.

"What happened?" Val asked. "Did a hidden nail get you?"

"No, but for some reason that spot suddenly got hot to the touch. Burning hot."

Val offered a skeptical look and placed her hand carefully on the same spot. "Not hot now. But my hand feels like it's glued down." Only with Ryder's help was she able to remove it.

I studied the finial, looking for some hidden compartment I'd missed when I removed it from the bag and handed it to Ryder. I'd noticed nothing at the time, but now that it was reattached, maybe I should check again. It didn't burn or pain my hand. Instead, a wave of nausea swept through me, forcing me to steady myself before I fell off the stairs.

"This is so weird," I said, stating the obvious to the other two. "It's like it's trying to tell us something."

"Like stay off me?" Val said.

I felt the rest of the railing, then the baluster and the treads and risers. Nothing. I tried the finial again. Same nausea as before.

Val and then Ryder repeated their actions with the same results.

"Do we need to call in an exorcist?" Val asked, only half joking.

"I have no idea," I replied. "I've never run into anything like this. Why do we each react differently?"

"Is it reading some kind of vibe within each of us?" Val asked.

Ryder rolled his eyes. "C'mon, ladies, you can't seriously be thinking this thing is, what? Spooked? You're letting your imaginations get carried away."

"You didn't imagine that heat coming through. But just for you. It changed its tune when it wouldn't release my hand," Val said.

"Seems like we either pull it off again or live with it and warn others not to touch it."

"Great selling point, Mom." She retrieved a chisel and attempted to pry the finial away from the newel post. It wouldn't budge.

"Looks like Plan B or some version of it will have to do. At least for now," I said, realizing I'd have to revise my thinking about haunted houses once again. The finial was something real, solid. To my surprise, I was ready to deal with that rather than some ethereal being. "I can't help thinking it's trying to tell us something. I know it's an inanimate object, but that's the best I can come up with. We may have solved the mystery of the midnight invaders, but now that this piece is back where it's been all along, I think we've learned this house really is haunted."

LATER THAT AFTERNOON, HAVING DECIDED TO PUT THE MYSTERY OF the finial on hold until we'd done more research, I returned home in search of a less weird environment. I'd barely set down my purse and notebook computer bag when Jason showed up in high Jason mode, circling my ankles repeatedly, sharing his silky softness.

"Look who's suddenly made himself available. You seem like your old self. How did that happen? I never gave you any of the meds Dr. Gardiner gave me." Then it came to me, although once the idea occurred, I wasn't sure I wanted to give it any credence. But if I followed Herc's example, I had to go with the evidence. And the evidence told me the only thing that had changed in the last twenty-four hours was the fact that the finial was no longer on-site.

It had taken longer than I anticipated to find the finial the day before. It was still in the canvas bag I'd thrown it into, but I must've tossed the bag way in the back of my larger closet, the one where I suspected Jason spent his time. Had the finial had a similar effect on my feline friend that it had exerted on Val, Ryder and me?

Maybe in the days ahead I'd consult some resources on unexplained phenomena, but for now, Jason appeared to be normal again, and that was our little secret.

In time, I hoped we could convince the finial we only meant the house well and we, the humans, and it, the chunk of wood, could coexist peacefully. I couldn't wait to challenge Val for which of us got to ask Amanda how she'd like to sell a haunted house.

AFTERWORD

Dear Reader,

Thank you for reading this book. If you liked it, won't you please take a minute to leave a review?

To keep up with Ro and Val's growing business and Ro's latest homicide case, sign up for my newsletter at https://www.subscribepage.com/BBCozies.

This is my second cozy mystery series. I've also written nine books in the Mah Jongg Mystery series. You can learn more about them and also the eleven contemporary romances I've published on my website, www.barbarabarrettbooks.com.

Follow me on:

- Facebook: http://bit.ly/2aXZvG9
- Twitter: https://twitter.com/bbarrettbooks

SNEAK PEEK
WRENCHED AT THE REINDEER RUN

**Excerpt from *Wrenched at the Reindeer Run*,
the seventh book in the
Nailed It Home Reno Mysteries series**

The marathon was to begin at seven. Short night, but I felt I should show up at least for part of it to show my support. Chuck would've gone with me, but he wanted to check the restaurant and wine bar to make sure the cleaning crew had put everything back in order and after that he planned to check in on Shane.

The run was to take place in Busse Park, a large plot of land donated to the city several years ago by an entrepreneur who'd made his fortune in early internet marketing and leveraged it into a monumental online magazine empire before selling it a few years ago and retiring to Fuji. He'd run high school races in the park as a boy and purportedly didn't want to see it sold off to developers once he left town. I didn't come here often, but it was a great place to sneak off to when I needed to think by myself.

I barely got inside the front entrance when I was stopped by a patrol car. "Sorry, ma'am. You can't go any farther."

Apparently she was a younger officer who didn't recognize me.

"I came to watch the race. Isn't there any visitor parking?"

"The race has been postponed indefinitely," she said tersely.

"Postponed? Why?"

She bit a lip, wanting to say more but held back by orders.

"It's okay to tell me. I'm Rowena Summerfield. Formerly Lieutenant Summerfield. I was a homicide detective for the city."

"Oh, Lieutenant Summerfield. I've heard about you. You still work with the force from time to time, right?"

I nodded.

"Are you here for the accident?"

I wanted to act like I was, but I didn't want to get this young woman in trouble. She seemed fairly new and a bit overwhelmed by the situation. "Accident? No, I just came to support the marathon. I was a volunteer at last night's Rendezvous."

"I'm not supposed to let anyone in that isn't here on official police business, but I can at least tell you. The main viewing stand collapsed. They think there was someone under it."

The viewing stand? Wasn't that the structure Adrian Seiser claimed he'd been working on? "That's horrible. Do they know who it was?"

She shook her head. "I just got here a little while ago. All I know is that it wasn't a runner."

My phone rang. She allowed me to pull off to the side to answer it.

"Did I interrupt your beauty sleep?" Herc asked, his typical way of greeting me when he called early in the morning. He knew better because I'm still an early riser, a habit that carried over from my days on the force.

There are so many possible replies to that question, but I think I've exhausted them over the years. "What's up?"

"Funny you should ask. Actually, not funny. That guy that caused last night's altercation, Seiser?"

"Yes?" I replied, my fingers tingling, knowing what was to come.

"He was in an accident here at the marathon. The whole

viewing stand collapsed on top of him. They just pulled out the body."

ACKNOWLEDGMENTS

This book would not have been possible without the input and suggestions of my editor, Chris Kridler, of Sky Diary Productions. Chris also produced the incredible cover, formatted the manuscript and put zip into the back cover blurb.

Thanks also to Harriet Sawyer, Bernadine Marsis and Judie Stark for their keen proofing eyes.

As always, thanks to my husband, Veryl, for his ongoing support.

BOOKS BY BARBARA BARRETT

Cozy Mysteries

The Mah Jongg Mystery Series

Craks in a Marriage

Bamboozled

Connect the Dots

Beware the East Wind

Flower Power

Jokers Wild

The Charleston Challenge

The Dragon Lady Gets Her Due

Courtesy Call

also available in paperback

Nailed It Home Reno Mysteries

Measure Twice, Murder Once

Loose Screw

Death by Drywall

Homicide by Hammer

Nuts and Bolts

Snared by the Snake

A LITTLE ABOUT
BARBARA BARRETT

Barbara Barrett started reading mysteries when she was pregnant with her first child to keep her mind off things like her changing body and food cravings. When she'd devoured as many Agatha Christies as she could find, she branched out to English village cozies and Ellery Queen.

Later, to avoid a midlife crisis, she began writing fiction at night when she wasn't at her day job in human resources for Iowa State Government. After releasing eleven full-length romance novels and two novellas, she returned to the cozy mystery genre, using one of her retirement pastimes, the game of mah jongg, as her inspiration. Not only has it been a great social outlet, it has also helped keep her mind active when not writing.

Though not an interior designer, that occupation has always fascinated Barbara. Her father was a carpenter and her husband has his own woodworking business. Exposure to their work got her interested in watching numerous home improvement shows on HGTV. Ro and Val are an amalgam of several HGTV hosts. Barbara used that combination of personality traits for Ro and turned her into a female sleuth who rehabs older houses.

Barbara is a member of Sisters in Crime, Sinc-Iowa and Florida Star Fiction Writers.

She is married to the man she met her senior year of college. They have two grown children, eight grandchildren and two great grandchildren.

Now retired, she is a resident of Florida, although she spends her summers in Iowa, her home state, and Minnesota. She earned her B.A. degree in History from the University of Iowa and her Master's Degree in History from Drake University.

When not in front of her laptop creating her next story, she plays mah jongg, watches TV detective shows and enjoys lunches with friends. Most recently, she has begun to paint in acrylics and is working to evolve her skills.

www.ingramcontent.com/pod-product-compliance
Lightning Source LLC
Chambersburg PA
CBHW061241210726
48293CB00003B/859